The Brighton Tarot Card Mystery

The Brighton Tarot Card Mystery

and Other Short Stories

NEALL RYON

A delightful romp through Brighton England with a self styled police detective on the trail of a dimutive thief and a mysterious deck of fortune telling tarot cards plus a dozen additional short stories, some taken from life and some are pure fiction.

Primix Publishing
East Brunswick Office Evolution
1 Tower Center Boulevard, Ste 1510
East Brunswick, NJ 08816
www.primixpublishing.com
Phone: 1-800-538-5788

Published by Primix Publishing: 11/26/2024

ISBN: 979-8-89194-346-9(sc)
ISBN: 979-8-89194-347-6(e)

Library of Congress Control Number: 2024920662

Dedication

This book is dedicated to the thousand and one teachers customers, and clients, who have complimented my written material many times over the years that I have been given a gift with an ability to clearly convey thoughts and ideas through my words A few of these individuals include Alan Hill; Poet Laureate, City of New Westminster BC, Author, Narrow Road to the Far East, Lavana LeBray Renaissance book Store New Westminster, BC, Deborah Kelly Poet, Author of Through My Eyes, Heartworks, Cry of Humanity, and several other published works.

Contents

The Brighton Tarot Card Mystery

The Theft

Helene yelled "Stop! Stop!" at the rapidly fleeing thief; "Stop him! Stop that thief! Stop him!" The man, or more likely a boy because of his diminutive size, was running at full tilt, clutching his prize to his chest. He flew down Western Avenue and the short distance to Dyke Street, onto North Road and then still running arrived at the next corner. Grasping the lamp post, he swung onto the cobblestones of Duke Lane. Checking behind him, he slowed to an easy jog and as he slowed his pace he calmed his breathing to be sure he would not be noticed. Tyler was still filled with the thrill and excitement of the snatch and run; he smiled and thought to himself; "That was much more fun than shoplifting. I should try that again."

By the time he got to Ship Street, he had slowed his pace to a walk and closed the fifty yards to the opening to Brighton's labyrinth of alleyways and lanes. The Lanes, as they are called, are remnants of England's medieval past with short narrow streets that are a maze of small merchants' shops, restaurants and stores. He entered Black

Lion Lane, A few more yards he turned left, walked past Zizzi's Greek restaurant, then made a quick right onto Prince Albert Street.

His instructions had been simple and clear. "Wait until the old woman is packing up her table and after she has put the cards into the box she will put the box on the table. Then she always turns and reaches for her knitting bag. You will strike at that exact moment; grab the box from the table and run like hell. Make sure you don't drop it or I will have your hide. Use the Lanes to make sure you are not followed and then come along Prince Albert to Kensington then head up towards Trafalgar. When I am sure you are not being followed I will let you find me. Now go!"

Tyler had been watching Helene's last customer get up from the folding chair, close and place it against the folding table that Helene used to do her Tarot readings. She was a frequent customer of Helene's and they chatted briefly before she left. Helene had worked this spot at the entrance to Churchill Mall since she began doing readings for public customers. She relied on her feelings to let her know when there weren't going to be more customers; besides, she had been feeling uneasy all afternoon. Something was not right so she was glad to quit and go back to her tiny apartment. Helene began to pack up her small street business. She collected the 21 cards that had been placed into a pyramid spread for the last reading and merged them into the single deck of cards, placing them carefully into the well-worn small box and then onto the table. Helene turned to reach for her knitting bag exactly as the dark-coated man had said.

Tyler had been waiting for this moment. He lept over the small retaining wall behind Helene's position, snatched the small box from the table and burst from the scene as though shot from a cannon. Passers-by turned to see the old woman shrieking; "Stop! Stop him! Stop that thief. Stop him!" The boy zigged and zagged through shoppers and strollers in the crowded street, leaping over intruding obstacles and skilfully avoiding the few stingy attempts to capture him. Within twenty steps he had reached the intersection of Western Road and Dyke Street and disappeared around the corner.

That small box contained Helene's pride and joy and her livelihood. These Tarot Cards had recently come to her through several strange coincidences. She was given the deck by a friend who had purchased it in a coffee shop in the adjoining city of Hove. The shop had originally been an antique and collectibles shop and the owner had decided it would make more money as a coffee shop filled with antique items that were also for sale. The owner, Tom Carlson, had found the Tarot deck in one of the drawers of a small cabinet of indeterminate vintage he had acquired in an estate sale. Tom was a retired business professional with little interest in anything esoteric and when his regular customer, Mary Travis told Tom she knew of someone this would be a perfect gift for, Tom accepted her £ 5 offer.

Helene had for a long time been interested in spiritualism, divination and any other forms of the occult that offered an escape from the mundane existence of knitting tea cozies and gossiping about the nearly dead or the newlywed with her local hag-pack as she called her friends. She immediately fell in love with the beautiful hand-painted deck and after a few weeks of intense study, she started offering free readings for her friends in the hag-pack. It was not long after, as her experience and knowledge of the patterns in the card grew that the magic began to happen. The results were often surprising, even startling. Her readings of future events of good fortune, ill health or other surprises and dangers for the querent who sought the advice, were increasingly accurate and her reputation grew. Helene realized this could be a source of revenue she bought a folding table and chairs so she could set up close to the entrance to Churchill mall, offering her readings.

Helene had one problem with the deck. The deck appeared to have two, too many cards. Helene's cards were a Rider-Waite-Smith deck which was supposed to have 78 cards; twenty-two Court cards, fourteen Wands, fourteen Cups, fourteen Pentacles and fourteen Swords. When the deck was examined face up the deck had the appropriate number of Court cards and suits.

One day the cards were spilled face down out across the floor. To confirm she had retrieved them all Helene counted them. Helene counted them leaving them face down. She counted 80 cards. This cannot be! The standard Rider-Waite Tarot deck has 78 cards. She counted them face down again she counted 80 cards, she counted the cards again placing the cards face up, the deck had the correct composition of cards but counted face down the deck always added to 80 cards. Try as she might she couldn't tell which of the cards were the two extra ones. When she tried again arranging them face up in their proper suits and Court cards fit perfectly into the correct pattern but no matter how many times Helene counted the cards when they were face down the total always came to 80 cards. "Impossible, she thought: Clearly something more than a little mysterious, and quite frankly impossible, is going on so there must be an explanation, but what could it be?"

The handoff

In the gathering gloom of the approaching evening, Tyler walked past George Ritter without noticing a dark-coated man standing inside a typical red English telephone booth. As he passed his patron of thievery, George stepped in behind Tyler and kept pace until Tyler, with a start, noticed the presence of someone behind him. Tyler's adrenalin sent a message to his legs to run but a hand on his shoulder restrained him and the voice attached to the hand spoke; "You have the package I sent you for?"

"Yes," Tyler answered.

"Give it to me!" the voice ordered.

Tyler turned to see a folded 20-pound note in one hand and an open gesture in the other. Tyler reached for the money which quickly withdrew. Understanding the meaning Tyler reached into a pocket inside his denim jacket. His Mom had sewn large pockets on the inside of his jacket without realizing they were his 'special' shoplifting pockets. He clutched at the box and handed it to George, grasping the £ 20 bank note.

"I will contact you again if I need your services," exclaimed George; "now get lost!"

Ms. Sincerity Black

Between 1815 and 1822 John Nash, Architect, designed and supervised the building of the Royal Pavilion in Brighton for England's King George IV. The exterior of the Pavilion was modelled in the style of the Mahal Palaces of the Royalty of India complete with towers, turrets, minarets and spires. Being a creative sort, Nash was able to scrounge or otherwise obtain enough minarets, towers turrets and spires to complete a miniature version of the Pavilion in the form of a four-story home for himself. As time wore on, ownership of the miniature castle changed and changed again and the property was eventually converted into flats with the uppermost garret level occupied by Ms. Sincerity Black.

The highly unusual *Arabian Nights'* appearance of this building very much suited Ms. Black who was a student of the occult. She was a tall, young woman, slim beyond slim and somewhat Gothic in both countenance and style. She saw herself as an empowered Master, a dominating creature able to enforce her will upon a compliant world. Yes, Ms. Black had a few minions that would gladly do her bidding but they were few in number and privately she thought of them as the worms from which her garden of willing thralls would grow.

When she was a teen, Ms. Black changed her name from Cynthia to Sincerity. She thought of herself as Sin, dropping the second and third syllables. To hide the change from her parents' Sin asked her friends to call her Cyn or Sin as she preferred to spell it. It had begun as a simple teen rebellion but Sin soon accepted herself as God's secret desire to be sinful once in a while and break free of the *'Goody-two-shoes'* image that people have of God. At least that is how she understood how Christians think of God.

Sin was happiest when she was ranting about something or someone. Her current target was the Christian beliefs of her parents. For Sin, Christian rules were too tight and surely God would blow a gasket if totally confined to 'Love and Kindness' all the time. "Maybe that's what war was all about," she thought; "God blowing a gasket!" The tension of God having to be perfect all the time with no way to blow off a little steam causes God to go on an occasional rampage. So He floods Bangladesh or Romania causing a few thousand people to drown or maybe He shoots a few hundred people for entertainment when He spends a weekend in Chicago. Let God throw a party in heaven once in a while, get a little drunk or some other mischief and the world will have lots less violence." Sin chuckled to herself thinking about God flirting with one of His Angels. "What an interesting conversation that would make."

"It is patently clear in this reality that the lion is never going to lay down with the lamb unless the lamb is lunch. Humans have always been mesmerized by pageantry and any church doctrine worth its' salt knows how to put on a good entertaining ritual to keep the masses hypnotized. Look a little deeper and it is easy to see the rituals and the stories told by men are intended to control the masses through fear and faerie tales. "Yes, yes! There's the answer." "Yes!" She concluded; "Control others through fear and faerie tales. What do I need to give me the power to survive in this thoroughly mixed up, insane world that I live in? I need power over others. How can I gain control over others?"

And thus began Sin's journey into the mysterious and secretive world of the Occult. She learned how to use her personality to charm, cajole, threaten, manipulate, overpower and control others.

Sin's Mother, who had survived the war in her home country, had learned well how to use her hidden anger, and her manipulation skills to survive. Without intending to harm her child, she wordlessly, through example, shared the hidden anger and the ability to promise the moon but only deliver more promises. Sin knew lots about the Tarot and loved that the interpretation could be manipulated. According to her a Tarot reading, if well-read, could foretell a coherent message of future events and reveal paths to good fortune or a direction to the healing of life's traumas. But while the Tarot cannot be manipulated the interpretation of the readings can be used to bend the truth of a reading in any direction. As the old adage says "A good liar can twist a story so that it looks appealing to the lazy, enticing to the ignorant, and powerful to the weak." It could also be said that the intention of a seeker, especially a seeker in physical or emotional pain can oftentimes be diverted from the truth by a few shiny baubles and a promise of relief. Sin had no guilt about using whatever interpretation that served her first and if it served the Querent, the customer, that was good, but first, it had to serve Sin and her agenda.

Word came to Sin about Helene and the amazingly clear and accurate readings she gave from a little folding table set up in the heart of Brighton's Churchill Square. Like the jealous witch in the Snow-White tale over 'Who is the fairest-in-the land?' Sin wanted to be seen as the true witch she imagined herself to be and sought to capture the power offered by knowing the future. Her jealousy was expressed as her determination that nobody was going to be better at predicting the future than her; "Especially better than that dumb old cow down at the Mall."

Sin picked up the phone and scrolled through the list; "Ah yes," she thought; George Ritter will be very willing to look after this for me.

Besides I'm sure he has more than a little larceny in his past. Sin selected the number and tapped; dial.

Raven's Shadow

George believed this was going to be like taking candy from a baby but now that he had the box of cards in his hands he felt a rush of excitement run through him. "I've got it! I've got it! Mistress will be so pleased. I am so pleased!" He hurried up Kensington Gardens toward Trafalgar Street.

Unusual as it was to find a Raven within a populated area; however, that point is irrelevant as George did not notice the large black bird perched atop the roof of the Easy News shop at the corner. Raven cocked his head slightly and watched George scurrying along the cobblestones towards Trafalgar Street. Raven watched and waited while George pulled out his mobile and made a phone call. He then walked quickly towards Queen's Road. Raven had flown to the top of the office building opposite the train station and the adjacent taxi stand. He watched as George entered a taxi that then pulled away and headed back towards Western Road. From his aerie perch, Raven caught glimpses of the cab as it moved westward across the city.

Raven fell directly downward from his high perch with wings folded and rapidly gained momentum enough to shoot him skyward when his wings opened. Moving westward across the sky, the Black Raven was joined by another Raven, a rare white Raven. Together swooping, diving and generally playing with the strong breeze off the ocean, the pair followed the course of the small red taxi. When the cab pulled up in front of the odd little building on Western Terrace the two separated and White Raven flew down to roost on a ledge of one of the turrets.

George Ritter got out, paid the driver and looked up at the building's upper turret. He was still excited but now that he was about to engage

Mistress Sin the feelings of excitement began the short transition to feelings of fear.

George was a little man. Physically in size, he would be considered average, but size doesn't make the man. Some would say that a man who has a sense of connectedness with himself, a vibration of completeness, a sense of knowing of one's place in his community and a willingness to connect with others are what makes up a man. George was a little man, with no friends to speak of, no interest in others and no interest in doing things, going places or participating in activities that would connect him to others.

George had a deep and unfulfilled need to be loved. Sin knew how to exploit this inner need in George and the others that she could control in varying degrees from a little to outright mastery. Mistress Sin didn't care about the source of this characteristic; she only wanted to exploit that need. George feared that if he didn't please her Sin would take away her love as a show of her displeasure. The pain would begin as a trickle of fear and could quickly grow to an excruciating pain of self-loathing. A pain George didn't notice was the same pain he felt when George's Mother withdrew her love as punishment. George was a little man. He was afraid not to be.

George entered the foyer of the building. He was slightly miffed the elevator wasn't waiting for him when he entered and as he knew Sin would be waiting he started up the stairs which wound their way up to the fourth-floor turret. Not a connoisseur of physical exercise, George was running short of breath as he reached access to Sin's apartment; The Crypta Sanctum, as she liked to call it.

George stopped to catch his breath. "What took you so long you good-for-nothing skiver?" You should have been here two minutes after I heard the cab door slam. You have it? Where is it! Give it to me!" George took the small box from his coat pocket. Sin snatched the box from George's hand and turning she stepped towards the window and the growing darkness of evening. Sin loved the night and the darkness it brought but her turning was mostly to deny George a chance to see the cards as she opened the box. George stood there patiently waiting for recognition for a job well done. Sin spoke mostly to herself as in her mind at that moment George had ceased to exist; "So the magical Tarot deck is mine. The deck that never hides the truth about light or darkness is mine. If this rumour is true and I can see into people's futures and know what will be. I will be powerful and I will be rich."

Totally focused on the box and its contents, Sin never noticed the rather large white bird perched on the railing of her balcony. Even if she had noticed she would have thought it only another seabird. After all, this was Brighton, a seaside community and it would never have entered the realm of possibility that this was a Raven, much less a white one.

Arthur the Coppa'

Arthur Tysdale had always wanted to be a Copper, a Bobby, a policeman. As a child Arthur daydreamed that he was Sherlock Homes or TV's ever-inquisitive Colombo solving crime through intelligent deduction without the guns and violence that is the hallmark of American television. Arthur worked mostly as a plainclothes police detective but Brighton\Hove was a small force and even after many years on the force he was often assigned the routine of a Uniformed Patrolman often directing traffic. His dearest dream was that someday he would be called to head up an investigation into a major case like the mysterious disappearance of the Crown Jewels from the Tower of London which he would quickly solve through his acute powers of deduction and his keen intuition. Arthur laughed at his daydream. "Still the boy dreaming about being a detective." he thought to himself.

While Arthur was explaining to an elderly motorist that parking was not allowed in a bus loading zone despite the fact there were no buses present, Arthur received the call of a reported robbery at Churchill Mall. His first thoughts were there had been a jewellery store heist or maybe they had cornered the man who had been shoplifting sexy underclothing from local Lingerie Shops. Arthur would have liked that but as he swiftly walked across the plaza at Churchill Square his excitement faded when he saw the old fortune-teller waving him over to the retaining wall at the entrance to the mall and her folding table.

Arthur's disappointment deepened as he learned about the snatch theft of a simple deck of Tarot cards from the old street vendor. "Hardly worth the trouble," he thought to himself; "Why do I always get the balmy ones?" Then aloud Arthur said; "Now then, what seems to be the trouble?"

Helene dove into a rant-filled tirade that contained every detail of the Great Tarot Robbery, which included the saga of her escape from Serbia with her Mother, the size of her small pension and why couldn't the country have better manners than to perpetrate such atrocities on little old ladies.

Amid the non-stop rant Arthur was able to get in a few short interjections; "Well, we will look into this matter. I assure you I will look into this. Yes; right away! Yes, I understand this is your only means of support apart from your too small pension. Yes, Madam. I understand these cards are special and are of vital importance to you. Yes Ma'am I will look into the matter.

Happy to get away, Arthur realized he would have to enter this in the incident book at the station but he was so in a hurry to escape that he didn't get Helene's last name and forgot to get a contact number. "I'll be damned if I'm going back there to get the details!" He thought to himself. With nothing particular to go on Arthur went back to his traffic duties but he couldn't stop thinking about the theft of a deck of Tarot cards. "Yes, a grab for cash but a box of cards? He had to have known it was a deck of some kind of playing cards and from the sound of his description, he was a street kid. Arthur continued with his musing; "Now, what would a street kid want with a box of playing cards? Who knows what a street kid would want with anything that couldn't be easily turned into cash and why am I giving this none-event any of my time? In the grand scheme of things, this is nothing, a nothing at all." Arthur's mind went from the words; "Why in hell am I bothering with this?" directly back to why would a street kid steal a deck of cards. "I mean, it's not like a picked pocket or anything of monetary value. And this kid did it in broad daylight with dozens of people around. There was an element of risk so there must be some value to those cards."

Arthur mused over many questions during his evening meal and into the evening. The fact he couldn't seem to shake the question out of his mind plus the story from Helene about the specialness of these cards had piqued Arthur's curiosity 'to make inquiries" as he had said to her. After all, he had promised Helene he would look into the matter. The next morning dressed as the plainclothes detective Arthur went back to Churchill Square to get the name, address and phone number details he had omitted yesterday. Arthur rationalized his attraction to this *non-event* robbery, as he put it, by saying he was doing a little PR with the public by showing Helene he was actually "Making inquiries."

Arthur left Helene offering Tarot readings with a recently acquired deck of cards from Waterstones bookstore just down the block. He trudged on up the street and absentmindedly turned onto Queen Street and headed up towards the train station. "Queen Street; ah yes, maybe the street kids up by the train station might shine a little light on the Great Tarot Theft Mystery," with a touch of sarcasm he chided himself for allowing this non-event theft to distract him.

A short time later, Arthur approached a group of street kids sitting on the benches between the bus terminal and the train station. "'Ello copper;" The homeless runaway from East London spoke up. "s'up, coppa. I swear I did'n' do it." and pointing to the kid next to him "'e did. Everyone broke into laughter with a little elbowing. Arthur joined in the laughter.

"I won't arrest him this time," Arthur chuckled as he leaned forward changing to a conspiratorial tone. "But I do have a question. Who is there amongst the street kids or local rag-tags would want to steal a deck of Tarot cards?"

"'old on coppa," the London kid interrupted, "what's a terra card? I ain't never 'eard o' terra. 'sept maybe for Molly's mum; now ain't she an 'oly terra?" This evoked more laughter and more jostling.

Realizing our young refugee from East London was the ringleader, Arthur continued the conspiratorial tone, looking back over his shoulder and then back to the boy. Quietly he asked; "What's your name son?"

"Roger and I ain't your flippin' son, coppa!"

"Well, Roger, I have this question and I don't know the answer because it just doesn't make a lot of sense to me. You seem like the man in the know around this group and I need your help. "Why would a street kid steal something that wasn't a good prospect to pawn?"

"I promise you coppa, what where there ain't no *bread an' 'oney* involved ain't no street kid do nuttin' for no-one but what it gets 'im some lucre."

Arthur understood the idiom "bread and honey" was a Cockney rhyming expression for money and sensing an opening, quickly pressed forward; "OK! So who's been flashing cash?"

"I'll 'ave a laugh! Flashing money! Us stree'ers together couldn't raise 'nough for a pack o' smokes and if we ever have a bit o'bread 'n 'oney people 'fink we stole it. 'Ell, just last night this kid from over 'ove had an 'ell of a time to trying to cash twenty quid some bloke gave him for running an errand. Nobody would, they all thawt' it was a phony. Finally, 'e 'ad to buy sumpin' from Tesco's. 'e said his Mom wanted some gum and some dim dolly believed 'im."

"What's his name?"

"'aven't a Scoobie! 'aven't a clue in your language."

A young girl, a streeter herself, had been listening; "We call him 'T'. We don't know his name. He don't hang around here much. He's a juvie." Arthur understood that to mean the boy is a juvenile but it could also mean this boy 'T' has been in trouble with local juvenile authorities.

"A last name?" Arthur looked hopefully at Roger, but Roger, after giving the girl who spoke up a nasty look, had obviously decided this, 'elping a coppa, had gone too far; so called for the group to move on. Ignoring Arthur's thank yous, the group disbursed and disappeared in less than a minute.

Arthur headed down to Western Road to catch a bus over to Hove and the Crown Prosecutors' office. Arthur made inquiries with the youth social worker at the CPS office and learned there were several prospects but the best description fit a boy named Tyler Moore who was known to social services for minor scrapes with the law. The cooperating counsellor gave Arthur access to Tyler Moore's file and photo and suggested Tyler might still have his part-time job as a gofer at a local Gym.

In 20 minutes, Arthur was standing face to face with a young Tyler Moore on the steps of Cheetahs Gym in Hove. Sensing an opportunity, Arthur decided on a surprise attack. "You're Tyler Moore?"

Tyler replied "Take a hike!"

Ignoring Tyler's rejection Arthur went on; "I'm detective Arthur Tysdale of the Brighton Constabulary. You can talk to me here or down at the nick. What's it going to be?

"Ok. What's the show about?"

Taking a chance he opened with an accusation; "I know you received at least 20 quid to run an errand for someone yesterday and I want you to tell me who it was that gave it to you."

Threatened, Tyler stepped back; "None o' your business."

Arthur drew himself up to his full height to increase the threat. "Look, here's your choice, you work with me or wind up in the lockup. I can prove you stole those cards from the old woman and you got a measly £ 20 for your trouble. You tell me who set you on that task or I'll make sure there's a lot more trouble coming your way. How about some time at Borstal for starters? A few years at training school should put you right."

Tyler couldn't keep the fear in him from growing louder and louder, keeping him from thinking how is it the copper knew it was he that stole the box? The fear of being locked up, even at a training school, convinced Tyler that Arthur had the goods on him.

"OK! OK! I doesn't know him from a hole in the ground. He just jumped me in the street and offered me twenty quid to grab a box from the old hawker in Churchill Square. I have no idea who he is. Ain't never seen him before." His frightened little boy nature took over and Tyler pleaded: "Please, I would like to help. I didn't hurt the old girl and I would give the box back to her if I could. I don't know anything 'cept what he told me to do. Wait until she was packing up, lift the box and meet him at Kensington between Gloucester and Trafalgar. The bloke scared me to death when he grabbed me from behind. I gave him the box and he gave me twenty quid."

After many more questions, Arthur had determined what the instigator, looked like, dressed like and the details of the hand-off. Several times he ran through the details of the exchange between the real criminal, whom Arthur decided, should temporarily be called Fagin after the Charles Dickens character.

On the walk up to Church Street to catch the number 26 bus back to Brighton and Churchill Square, Arthur's mind dragged him through several dead ends thinking about the interaction between the Fagin in this mystery and his underage errand boy.

"After the handoff how did they part? Tyler had headed south, back towards where he had entered the mews, which means Fagin headed north towards Trafalgar Street. Kensington dead ends at Trafalgar so where then did he go? What's up at Trafalgar Street? If he went east he would cross Pavilion Gardens, the Government buildings and, Ah yes, the Police Headquarters building. So let's assume he travelled west, what's west? It's a short walk to Queen Street, the railroad station the bus terminal and ... and in between a taxi stand. Is it possible he took a taxi?

Following the path Tyler had described, Arthur made his way to Kensington and then up to Trafalgar Street. Arthur walked west on Trafalgar and at Queen Street walked directly into the Taxis lined up for fares at the train station. "How convenient." thought Arthur.

Several taxis waited for their passengers and a clutch of drivers stood near the first car chatting and grabbing a quick smoke. Arthur asked them if anyone recognized a passenger of Fagin's description late yesterday. Although none did, they were willing to help and would ask other drivers.

"That's the end of it," thought Arthur, "I've wasted, far too much time on this already. Besides, there's a long way from finding our *Fagin* and proving he has the Tarot deck. This is a simple snatch and run, but for the life of me, I can't understand why. For less than £20 quid I can buy a brand new deck of Tarot cards from Waterstones Book Store just around the corner from Helene's table.

"And speaking of why; why in hell am I still wasting my day over a simple snatch and run theft; time to let it go. Let's get back to the beat." Paying no attention to this admonition and instruction to let it go, Arthur walked down Queen Street, as his mind wandered back to the Tarot deck. "Are these cards so special that someone went to so much trouble and expense to get this specific one?" He mused; "I wonder if the old girl can add anything to the story."

Pixies Two Cards

"Do you believe in magic? Helene asked Arthur who thought for a moment and replied. "Well no, not exactly. There are many things we don't understand or can't explain; but magic, I don't think I can say I believe in it."

Helene looked at him sadly; "Of course not! You're a policeman and you pretend to know only know what you know and nothing more. Well, this Tarot deck was more than a little special. I would say even magical. The readings from this deck were always 100% accurate. They never failed to tell the future and it often told the querent what might be done to undo a negative prediction and turn it to a positive outcome. These cards were an energy unto themselves and I was becoming a local celebrity for the readings I've been giving. Well, they're not exactly; my readings but expressions of love in the form of advice the cards always offered to the querent; the person that asks for a reading.”

“The cards know the future and I was so pleased with myself and busy doing readings that I didn't pay any attention to the warnings the cards were giving me that I was about to lose something of great value.”

“So who is there among others of the senior's community is there that might envy your growing reputation.”

“There's no one I know of. I don't hang out with those balmy old cabbages anyway.”

Arthur laughed as he remembered calling Helene a balmy old girl.

Helene lowered her voice and a serious look crossed her face; “I tell you, this deck is haunted by the ghost of Pixie Smith. She is, or was, the artist who, along with advice from the occult expert Arthur Waite the card's original designer. There are 78 cards to a normal store-bought deck, but these are special. I think Pixie may have designed 80 cards and the two missing cards are somewhere in that deck. There has to be some kind of mystical energy that's been added to those cards. Maybe it is Pixie herself because I'm beginning to believe this might be the original deck, hand-painted by Pixie herself. Maybe that's how those cards can see so clearly into the future.

Helene and Arthur chatted for a little while longer about Tarot and the mystery deck. She explained that counted one way; that is, face up they always add to 78 cards and there always were the correct distributions of suits but counted face down they always added to 80 cards. Arthur spoke his thoughts aloud; “If this is correct then this really is a mystery and as well, I now have a motive for the *actus reus,* the theft.”

Needing to understand more about this story Arthur excused himself and walked the short distance up Queen's Rd. and across North Street to the Jubilee Library. With internet access, Arthur searched for Pixie Smith and Tarot cards. Wikipedia offered the following information;

Until the publication of the Rider-Waite-Smith Deck in 1909 most Tarot cards were quite simplistic in design. Arthur Edward Waite, principal designer of the RWS deck, born in 1857 was a mystic and an occultist who was extensively involved in the study of all manner of esoteric matter. Waite joined the Order of the Golden Dawn and became a high-ranking Freemason in 1891. Waite was also a respected author and wrote several books on esoteric and metaphysical studies and became the revisionist founder of the New Order of The Golden Dawn. He was greatly interested in The Kabbalah, alchemy and equipped with his in-depth knowledge of the occult and esoteric symbolism he began the design of a definitive occult arts deck of Tarot cards. Pamela Colman-Smith was also deeply interested in the occult and became a member of the occult-based New Order of The Golden Dawn where she was introduced to Arthur Waite. Pamela (Pixie to her friends) was an artist, illustrator and writer who produced several books including; Widdicombe Fair and The Golden Vanity. She also wrote and illustrated books with stories from Jamaican folklore. As well, Colman Smith also provided illustrations for the Irish poet William Butler Yeats and illustrated Bram Stoker's novel, 'Lair of the White Worm'. Smith was born near London, in February 1878 to an American-born father and an English mother. Her family moved frequently from London to Manchester, to Kingston, Jamaica, then on to New York.

Pixie was a graduate of The Pratt Institute of Brooklyn N.Y., as an illustrator with education in theatre costume and set design. In 1909 Waite commissioned her to draw the imagery for a deck of Tarot that would be very different from previous decks.

It is believed that Waite provided Smith with detailed design themes for the Major Arcana as they were his main concern. For the Minor Arcana, she received a list of simple meanings from which she was to intuitively design the imagery herself. Smith drew on her imagination and background experience in theatrical design to create the wonderfully detailed and descriptive images of The Four Suits that are widely recognized today. The Rider-Waite-Smith Tarot Deck was introduced as having 78 cards but Smith claimed to have produced 80 cards. The Smith estate provided the original artwork of the 78 cards that became the Rider-Waite-Smith Deck; however, the missing two cards have never been found.

Damn it!" thought Arthur; no wonder I can't let this case drop. It's got a hold on me. It's wanting me to solve this who-done-it. Well Pixie, I'm in." As he left the library Arthur noticed a white bird roosting on the uppermost railing at the top of the building. What he didn't notice was the large white bird was not a commonplace seashore gull plentiful in seaside Brighton.

Not sure of the next step Arthur headed over to the taxi stand. Again he asked the assembled drivers if anyone had picked up a fare of the description Tyler had given to Arthur. Arthur had posted a note at the main taxi terminal asking for information about the mystery man but no new information had emerged so far. Arthur didn't notice the sound of Raven's croak. A driver spoke up. "You know, Charlie Mercer has been off since and he often parks here. Why don't you check with the office for his number? Give him a ring."

Believing it was a complete waste of time, Arthur phoned the number he was given. While Charlie didn't have a passenger of that description, he suggested that Ralph Rattray was also working that afternoon and might have. Still believing this was going to be another dead end, Arthur was sure there was no good reason to call Rattray. This time Arthur noticed the sound of a cawing and noticed the black bird sitting on the fence opposite the driver's centre.

"Was that a crow? That bird seems awful big for a crow but what in hell would a Raven be doing this far from the wood? "

"Hello Ralph Rattray, I am Constable Arthur Tysdale of the Brighton\ Hove Constabulary. I was wondering if you remember picking up a fare at the Train Station Taxi stand." Over the phone, Arthur proceeded to give the details of the suspect but before he could finish Rattray interrupted; "coat too warm for the mildness of the day and a wide-brimmed hat that partially concealed his face. Of course, I remembered. That one looked like he was up to no good."

"Yes, that sounds like our man. Do you remember where you dropped him off?" Again Rattray interrupted; "Not exactly but the trip sheet will have it. I go to work at 4 today, so meet me at the terminal and I will give you the exact address where I dropped him. Clutching a piece of paper, Rattray met Arthur with an address on Western Terrace just off Western Road. Come on, I'll take you there.

A short while later and after a taxi ride to the address on Western Terrace Arthur stood on the sidewalk looking up at the strange structure. The voice behind him said; "Your lordship that will be Four Pounds Forty."

Arthur laughed; "I thought you said you were going to take me to this address. I assumed that was going to be without charge."

"I did bring you here as I said, so now you owe me Four Pounds forty.

"Bugger!" remarked Arthur. Not too loudly so passers-by wouldn't hear.

"My, my," said the cabbie.

Arthur handed over a 5 Pound note; "Keep the change." and turned back to the white mini-palace. Behind Arthur, the cabbie waved a small piece of paper; "Your receipt, 'squire." Arthur wanted to ignore the proffered receipt but the cabbie let go of the paper which then fluttered to the sidewalk as he drove away. Unwilling to appear environmentally insensitive Arthur muttered another swear word under his breath and bend to pick up the paper. He absent-mindedly stuffed it into his coat pocket.

Arthur entered the building. There was no directory, just two doors, and a raising stairwell. "Where to start?" Arthur mused. It was either the door marked Apartment 1 or the other marked Elevator. Arthur knocked.

A female voice answered; "Who is it?" "I am a police officer madam, just a routine inquiry." The door opened. A short, elderly woman dressed with coat and hat on, opened the door. Holding up his Warrant Card, Arthur was about to speak when the woman turned her head towards the interior: "I must be going, Margaret. My! My! There's a nice-looking policeman, here for you. If you find out here's single tell him I just might have done it and give him my address." With that and a pleasant smile, the woman gently laid the fingers of a gloved hand on Arthur's arm as she exited past Arthur and out the main door. She was replaced by another middle-aged woman at the door to apartment one; "How can I help you, officer?

Still holding up his Warrant Card Arthur answered; "Police officer Madam, I am looking for a man about medium height who was seen entering this building yesterday evening at dusk. He was wearing a dark-coloured coat and hat."

"Oh, that would be a friend of Miss dark, mysterious-and-not-so-friendly, what lives up in the turret."

This reply stirred Arthur's interest. "What is there that brings you to give her that name?"

"Oh her and her cultish friends; I can smell the incense all the way down here, and the comings and goings at all hours. They must be up to no good. I tell you the young of this country have been spoiled rotten."

"Yes Ma'am that may be so but tell me about this woman. Her proper name for starters?

"Well, I only know she was introduced to me as Ms. Black, but," The woman lowered her tone as if sharing a secret; "I swear I heard one of her friends call her Sin, probably short for Cynthia or the like, but really!. I wouldn't allow my daughter's friends to shorten her name to Sin.

"Enough!" thought Arthur; "time to check this out." He spoke; "Well, thank you, ma'am it's really a man that I am making inquiries about. As Arthur turned to leave, he thought: "That should shake her off the scent." Those thoughts were dashed, as the woman was closing the door, she spoke out. "Well, you're not much of a Bobby if you don't visit Ms. Black up in the turret."

Arthur decided to take the stairs as his thoughts needed processing. "I'm in a lot of trouble! Arthur thought; "I think I've found our culprits but if I bring this case to the crown I may have difficulty proving this was Helene's Tarot deck. Hell, I may never get a court order to search and find the evidence. "Yes Your Lordship, I want a court order to find an irreplaceable deck of Tarot cards valued at £ 5.00. I might get off with a major scolding about wasting the courts' time. Maybe I can use the counting method to prove this deck is unusual but any magistrate worthy of his robes would suggest the counting was a parlour trick. Besides this was a theft of an item of only five quid and the crown prosecutor would refuse to clog up the courts with a minor case like this. It's not as though this is a ring of thieves with a ton of stolen goods. My best guess is to frighten the hell out of them. If I threaten to charge them with possession of stolen goods and as many other charges I can think of; corruption of a minor, conspiracy to commit a crime, conspiracy to corrupt a minor, conspiracy to corrupt a minor into committing a robbery. Arthur had reached the top step and took a minute to calm his breath. He knocked.

"Good afternoon, are you Ms. Black?"

Looking somewhat surprised; "Yes, who are you?"

"I am police constable Arthur Tysdale." He flashed his Warrant card; "May I come in?" He asked as he began to move to enter the apartment. Without hesitating he asked; "I am making inquiries about a man involved in a theft. He was seen entering this building yesterday evening."

A bolt of electricity shot through Sin's mind which was in a-whirl with thoughts. Her face betrayed her. First, it was a look of surprise quickly followed by the look of fear which reddened to show anger; "This can't be about the cards." she thought. "Is he talking about George? He has to be!! George, that fat pig, I'll kill him!"

The truth of this emotional display registered in Arthur's mind and he knew this was the right place and this was the right person.

"Well as you can see there's no one here but me." Sin said in a sweeping gesture with her arm. Arthur's eyes followed the gesture; noting, the Moon Star tapestry that hung on the wall, the mantle strewn with crystals and candles and an incense burner on the side table. He stepped further into the room. "I see you're interested in *les arts ésotériques* the yogic side or the occult?"

The 10-year-old detective inside of Arthur found his groove and the word games began.

Looking around Arthur spies a small table draped with a zodiac sun table cover. "You do Astrology readings?" Arthur asked.

"How dare he!" Sin thought; "I'm much better than any lowly planet pusher. No, I'm a psychic and a futurist. I use many tools that foretell future events."

What do you do? How do you see into the future; Crystal ball?

"Among other tools.

"Would that include the Tarot?" Arthur asked as he moved toward the old fashion divan that rested on carved claw feet. "Tarot has recently come to be of interest to me. Do you include Tarot in your toolbox?

"Well look, I'm very busy and as you can see there is no man here so I think it's time for you to leave."

Instead of heading to leave, Arthur slowly walked to the draped table, pulled back a chair and proceeded to seat himself. As he sat he motioned for Sin to sit in the chair opposite. "Well, I think you might know this man and perhaps you can give me his name if I describe him to you. He's wanted on several serious charges, among them theft, conspiracy to commit a crime, conspiracy to corrupt a minor, conspiracy to corrupt a minor into committing a robbery. And because he tutored a minor into committing a robbery he will be up for some serious jail time. This will not only cost him some jail time and also his accomplices as well. Serious jail time!" emphasizing the latter statement.

"We've tracked down the boy he paid to commit the crime and he'll be happy to identify this man so he can escape juvenile. I have an excellent description of the stooge who did this and I suspect he will turn in any others faster than you can say *Jack Robinson.*"

Arthur saw a flicker of fear as Sin approached the table. "What was stolen may I ask?"

"Nothing expensive, just a deck of Tarot cards, but the fact it involves a child makes it a most serious crime. I know the magistrate comes down heavy on those involved in corrupting minors and I expect he will come down hard on all those involved." Arthur knew the effect his threat was having as he changed to an emphasizing tone adding; "Seriously hard!"

Sin stood silent for several minutes considering her options. "A boy you say. A young boy? A teenager? That's terrible!" she remarked as she slowly took a seat opposite Arthur.

"No. Not a teenager but a preteen. A twelve-year-old, really still a child. Although children grow up so fast, but still" Arthur paused. "I'm sure the magistrate will see him as a child. The corruption of a child is a very serious offence meaning jail time for sure."

The idea of being locked up and in the control of others was an abhorrent thought to Sin. She saw there was an opening that if taken now might allow her to escape that fate. "OK," Sin started "I may know something about this theft but I want you to know I had nothing to do with it. I have them. I think I may have the cards that you say were stolen. They were a gift from George; George Ritter. He's an admirer of mine, more of an acquaintance. He gave them to me." Doing her best to portray a sense of innocence on her face; "I had no idea they were stolen."

Sin got up to take the box of Tarot cards from the drawer of the side table. "Excellent, I am pleased this matter has been concluded so quickly and because you cooperated so freely it is unlikely there will be further repercussions for you other than to testify if your accomplice, I mean if Ritter comes to trial. Mind you this whole matter might be reduced to a summary offence which would mean a fine and maybe some probation time. As the goods were returned this might turn out to have a less than dramatic ending."

"I want the details about this Mr. Ritter and yours as well." After making his notes, Arthur picked up the box and headed towards the door. "Thank you for your cooperation, Ms. Black. You did the right thing and because of your cooperation it is possible there will unlikely be any serious consequences for you but you might be wise to choose your friends more carefully."

Arthur entered the details of the theft and recovery into the Incident Report Ledger. He contacted George Ritter and had him come to the police station and admonished him severely for his folly. Arthur threatened him several times in several ways about pursuing all manner of charges if his name ever came up again.

The Final Reading

Helene was ecstatic at having recovered her cards and invited Arthur to her small flat for the express purpose of giving Arthur the first reading following the recovery of the cards. After tea was made and poured, Helene shuffled the deck while they chatted about the events of the past few days. Eventually, it was time for Helene to do her reading for Arthur. She shuffled then dealt out three cards laid out in a row, each one below the next one; the initial part of the six-card pattern in the form of a cross. As she dealt the cards she identified them by their names and explained their primary characteristic.

"The Hierophant; the keeper of all rituals and things sacred; access to the Akashic records; the compendium of all knowledge both undisguised and mystical that is encoded in the non-physical plane of existence known to the occult community as the astral plane."

She laid down the next card sideways across the first; "The Magician, the deceiver who hides the truth of this existence in plain sight behind the illusion that we identify as reality.

Helene dealt out the third card and placed it as the topmost card. "Death; Death is the origin and the dissolution of all things, the beginning of all and its ending. All in the Universe that exists comes to us from the place we call Death eventually returning to Death. Everything that exists is born and dies a thousand times each day but there is no such thing as a final Death. The energy of the Universe is constant and eternal.

Again Helene carefully laid out the fourth card at the bottom with the previously lain cards; "The Fool", Helene continued, "The Fool refuses to open his eyes to the beauty that surrounds us and sustains us. The Fool is afraid to ask the question, 'What is this energy that permeates all and sustains all?' The person who denies or fails to appreciate the amazing grace by which we live is The Fool."

Helene flipped over the next card and gasped. She had never seen this card before. It was a soaring, White Raven on a star-filled night sky facing the right side of the card. With a look of astonishment on her face, Helene placed this fifth card next to the left of the Magician.

As the sixth card was revealed, Helene gasped again. It was a Black Raven, swooping through a sunlit blue sky, its position facing left. Helene then laid this last card to the right of the Magician. Helene closed her eyes and placed her left hand over the White Raven card. She breathed in deeply and placed her right hand over the Black Raven card. Again a deep breath, her face mellowed, all wrinkles and traces of age left her face which now shone with peaceful stillness.

Helene's eyes remained closed, but as she spoke there was a change in her manner of speaking. It sounded as though she was speaking from some distance. Also, her broad Midlands accent had shifted to a mixture of English and American with a slight Jamaican lilt;

"I am the White Raven, I am the masculine principle. My name is 'The Law of One.' The Law of One is comprised of all that exists as it shares the same source and is thereby connected to all else that exists. All substance is, not an interconnected web or continuous chain but one entity comprised of all that is seen to exist or not. Together we form one living thing, the Universe. We are one. It is the law. The Law of One.

Again there was a silent pause, a deep breath, then the voice continued; "I am Black Raven. I am the feminine principle. My name is 'The Law of Many'. The Law of Many dictates that everything is alive and vibrating. All is conscious at every level of existence. All in existence in the Universe is composed of the collective vibration of each individual particle so that all matter is made up of discrete particles; each of which is conscious and aware.

We are, as is everything within the Universe, vibrating light manifest as matter. Whatever vibration you hold, be it positive or negative, the Universe will manifest an experience to match the vibration that you emanate. It is the law. The Law of Many."

The voice spoke one last time; "We are complete."

Then there was silence. It felt as though the silence would last an eternity. Neither Helene nor Arthur dared speak and break the spell woven by the voice that could only have come from Pixie. After a long silent pause, Helene opened her eyes, blinked several times and politely cleared her throat. With her normal English accent, she spoke: "The reading is complete."

Helene had the feeling that the mystery of the two cards was also complete. After another long silence and with a sense of sadness she began to pick up the cards. She knew this was the last time she would see Pixie's two missing cards again. It wasn't that she thought about it. She just knew that the next counting of the cards face up or face down would always add up to 78 cards.

The Ravens had brought their message and Miss Pixie's journey was now complete. Those that were omitted from the original desk had been denied expression of their message about the true nature of the Universe. Pamela Colman Smith could now rest in peace.

Arthur also knew the mystery was solved and indeed no longer existed. He rejected the urge to count the cards again. The case was not only closed, Arthur felt as though the past two days were days out of time. It was like he had dreamed the events. But that could not be the case. As Arthur put on his coat to leave, he thought to himself; "It all seemed so real. It; .. Arthur interrupted himself as he drew a small piece of paper from his pocket; "and besides if it wasn't real, where did this Four Pounds Forty cab receipt come from."

Brighton Beach

(This story is fictional and any resemblance to persons living or dead is purely coincidental.)

Chapter One

The clouds had rolled in sometime about noon along with the rising wind. There was nothing particularly ominous in the weather forecast; it was just another storm off the ocean bringing lots of rain and high winds. By 2 PM the gale warning flags had been raised at the marina and along the beachfront and by nightfall the wind from the southwest and the incoming tide caused the ocean to come crashing against the shore in powerful turbulent waves.

The sea would draw back from the shoreline retreating down the slope of the beach before cresting to a height of 10 to 12 feet then exploding onto the beach with a roar. Along with the thunder of the cascading water was the clatter of the stones and gravel that the receding wave had picked up to throw back onto the beach.

The seaside boardwalk was almost deserted as nightfall further darkened the sky. The wind and the stinging rain lashed at the few walkers brave enough to challenge the storm and if the wind didn't rip the umbrella out of your hands and send it skipping along the promenade, it would flip it inside out pulling the struts irreparably out of their sockets.

The boardwalk along the seafront also serves as the roof of the beach-level shops and gives pedestrians a degree of safety from the raging sea. But down at the eastern end, past where the Beach Hut Café marks the end of the boardwalk, the beach is made up mostly of gravel-sized stones and declines more steeply to the sea. This short stretch of shoreline lies between two piers that offer a great place to greet the incoming waves up close. These manmade barriers called groynes, jut out into the sea to protect the beach from erosion. They also create a perfect entrapment for waves that can rise to 20 feet or more before crashing onto the beach.

The boys; Dave Bartlett and his friend Roddy McClure were locals, and that evening they delighted in chasing the retreating waves as the water, stones and seafoam withdrew downward. The ocean would then cascade against the beach in thunderous breakers that chased the pair back up to safer ground. They were laughing and daring the sea to capture them running back and forth as the sea rose and fell.

The exhilarating power of the storm added to the feelings of excitement that the two teens shared. As well, the thrill of the challenge was heightened by the danger posed by the occasional double wave which didn't wait for the sea to draw back but pushed over the previous wave driving faster and higher up the beach.

In the darkness and the driving rain, Dave didn't see it coming. The intensity of the storm along with the surging tide drove a huge wave along the barrier wall and up the beach that caught Dave unawares. The wave knocked him over backwards in an explosion of seawater, foam and gravel.

As the retreating wave dragged him down the beach, Dave struggled to roll over and scramble to safety. A second wave struck him that carried him up the beach a short way but before he could get his feet onto something solid it retreated dragging him back into the roiling sea.

For a few seconds, Dave rose to the surface gasping for air and flailing his arms in a swimming motion, desperately trying to reach the beach and escape the churning sea. This next wave pulled back and as it surged forward, lifted the boy in a summersault motion to smash him face-first into the rocky shore. Again the sea drew back picking up the limp, unconscious body in a soup of saltwater, stones and seafoam. Another wave crashed forward and again tumbled Dave's body over and over as it climbed the slope, relentlessly dragging him back as the sea receded.

Roddy began a futile attempt at rescuing Dave. Wading nearly to his knees he almost fell over backwards as the receding wave pulled at the loose stones underneath his feet. The powerful wind was spitting foam off the crest of the next wave as it reared and began coursing its way along the groyne ready to leap up onto the beach. Roddy realized that he dare not challenge the raging sea further and escaped to higher ground.

He watched helplessly for a few minutes hoping Dave would miraculously save himself but realizing he could not help his friend he turned on the run to get help. The sea rose and fell rose and fell as the drowned boy was inexorably carried deeper and deeper into the turbulent water until he disappeared.

Chapter Two

Dave saw a body a few feet below him rising and falling with the surging waters. "Oh shite; this is bloody awful!" he thought; "That dumb bloke needs help or he'll drown." He watched the body; arms outstretched floating in the silent restless water, making no effort to save itself.

Spurred on by the storm-driven sea the body rolled over and as it turned toward him Dave recognized the face as his own. The face was calm, the body serenely floating in unison with the surging unrest of the storm and the sea. The physical entity that was once Dave Bartlett moved unresisting with the motion of the sea, no longer aware, but the conscious part that knew itself as David; the part that he thought could only come from within a living, breathing human body, was fully present. Dave watched the body that had been his, slowly but steadily fall away, further and further into the cold, dark, dispassionate sea.

It was then that Dave became aware of the total darkness. He still felt that he was moving, surging with the rise and fall of the sea, but with no reference point, only total darkness, he couldn't be sure. Dave considered what was happening and thought; "This is death. But I feel so solid, so calm. I'm still here." He pondered the idea of 'here'; "But where is here?"

He then noticed a noise that sounded like wind. Not the gentle whisper of wind through the trees but a shrill sound like metal wheels against a steel rail. It seemed to be coming from a tiny sparkle of light that had appeared beneath him. As the light grew larger and larger Dave wondered if the light was approaching him or was he falling into it. Against a completely black horizon, the sparkling light grew ever larger, increasing in speed as it approached him. And as it did the sound grew louder and louder until it was screaming inside his thoughts.

Suddenly, a white brightness enveloped him and the black horizon was vanquished. Just as suddenly, the intense noise stopped; replaced by complete silence. Dave, or perhaps only a thought that once was Dave, had emerged into shadowless, bright white light.

In this fog of whiteness, there was no sensation of hot or cold, no sound, no sensation of struggling to breathe and no pain from the physical damage done when he was smashed face-first into the stony beach. As well, there was no identifiable light source, just intensely bright, shadowless whiteness. He thought this absence of sensation should have been upsetting, but as he tested his emotions the only sensation he was feeling was a sense of peace; a quiet knowing that all is well.

Chapter Three

"How is this possible? Is this death? Am I dreaming? Hello!" he thought. "Hello? Is this heaven? Am I dead? Dave paused when he realized this was a dead man asking questions. "If so, how is it that I am asking these questions?"

A strong feeling of positive energy swept through him as he became aware of the presence of a distinct energy close to him. A disembodied energy appeared directly to Dave as a thought; "Welcome home." Came the words

"Home?" Dave could feel the new energy emitted a loving intent but there was no physical entity present that he could see. "Ah, yes!" the energy spoke; "Your ability to see non-corporeal energy has not caught up with you yet. Here, let me manifest physically so you can perceive me.

We are in the etheric realm."

The shadowless whiteness was replaced by a scene from Dave's memory of rolling grassed hills with occasional patches of green-leaved trees under an almost cloudless blue sky. A softly glowing form resembling the size and shape of a human appeared standing a short distance away. The voice of the spirit appeared directly as a thought; "Again, Welcome home."

Dave thought the question; "Am I dead?"

Again words were not spoken but Dave heard a reply. "Yes, you have discarded the physically manifested part of you that you called your body but that was only the vehicle that was required to carry the eternal part of you. This remaining non-corporeal part of you is your soul. This part of you is eternal; was never born nor will it ever die."

"Are you God?"

"All is God. God is not a separate being but what you refer to as God is the combined energy of everything in the Universe. God is the Universe, the total sum of all energies in all levels of existence including the levels where nothing appears to exist, such as this one. To put it briefly; God is the total of all energy that exists including you." The spirit paused a moment so Dave could digest these ideas. Then it continued; "So as I said; welcome home. Welcome home to your true nature.

The Trial

Tap, tap; "Is this mike on? Hi! Morley Shaver here; Welcome to, 'Evolution Observer' where we report news and views on the evolution of the Universe. We are here today in the Etheric realm where souls awaiting birth or rebirth design the life they think will add the experiences that will increase the Universe's awareness of its infinite self.

"Today we are reporting to you from The High Court of Universal Justice where we are witnessing the conclusion of a trial of stunning significance. A soul has petitioned the court to terminate the fetus to which he has been assigned in favour of a different parental coupling. The plaintiff is asking to experience a life assignment of greater potential to make a contribution of value instead of; as the soul described it, a life as fodder for the continuing procreation of low functioning masses."

"The other side is the defendant; Eve Knebworth, who is nine weeks pregnant with the incarnate to which the plaintiff has been assigned. She and Adam Knebworth, live within space-time and have testified they are

delighted to find themselves about to bring a child into the world. They find the request to abort the child outrageous.

"Documents previously submitted included all relevant details and we are here at the final hearing stage where both plaintiff and defendant will offer final arguments with their respective positions before the High Courts' Justice Solomon.

Court is about to convene. I will leave this microphone on so we can listen in."

The Injunction

"All rise; The High Court of Universal Justice is now in session; The All Compassionate Lord Solomon presiding."

Solomon, clothed in red velvet robes trimmed in ermine, mounted the bench and spoke in a voice that sounded like distant thunder: "Bailiff! Please read the requested injunction."

The Bailiff, a robed, grey-haired imaginary energy stood: "Your honour it reads, 'a Soul assigned to a developing embryo has requested the court to direct the carrier of the unborn, defendant, Eve Knebworth, residing within space/time, to abort her pregnancy and that the Plaintive be assigned to parentage of a greater potential for influencing the growth of awareness, love and compassion within their progeny'."

Solomon interrupted; "How is the soul plaintiff to be known?"

Counsel for the defendant stood: "Your Honourable Compassionate One, I am Olivia Cromwell, counsel for defendant Knebworth. My client is aware of the child's gender and has named him; Knoll Knebworth, nicknamed, Tobee." Ms. Cromwell continued; "I respectfully submit the defendant vehemently opposes the imposition of such an order and it is her intention is to carry her impregnation to term.”

Solomon held up his hand indicating stop; “Advocate please be seated.” and with a nod from Solomon, the Bailiff continued; “The defendant opposes the imposition of such an order from the court on the grounds that she has an unassailable right to motherhood.”

Solomon spoke; “Thank you, Bailiff. Will the Court Advocate please confirm the applicable Universal law as regards this injunction?”

The Court Advocate, a bespectacled, middle-aged, female energy stood; “Your Lordship there are two compulsory rules that apply. Universal proclamations state that all persons in the space-time continuum have dominion over all aspects concerning their physical bodies. Specific to this injunction, females are masters of their bodies and no external circumstances exist under which they can be compelled to act.

“Regarding the plaintiff, Universal Law states that humans in space-time have the right to manifest a happy, fulfilling life. The plaintiff claims that right by requesting to participate in the parental selection and engender a life of greater potential happiness resulting in a positive contribution to Universal Consciousness.

Court Advocate continued; “In conclusion, whereas litigants are both claiming constitutional rights, this case is; *est officio judici*, meaning it is the obligation of the court to render a decision.”

Solomon pondered this information for some time then spoke; “Thank you Advocate; Court will now hear arguments from the litigants. Plaintive first, followed by the defendant. Soul Tobee please proceed.”

The Plaintiff;

Tobee, a soul of unconsolidated energy arose; "Thank you, Lordship. There are more than my and the defendants' rights here at play. Yes, my incarnation into physical form will satisfy Mrs. Knebworths need to procreate but what of the rights of the unborn. Who speaks for the newborn's right to enter space-time into a nurturing, loving safe environment that will foster and support a life of happiness and fulfillment? On behalf of all children, I claim the right to a productive life intending to bring peace and creativity into a world suffering greatly from physical and emotional pain, acts of war, unthinkable violence and untimely death.

"Previously provided evidence of an unhealthy environment foretells the Knebworth's alcoholic, emotionally dysfunctional lifestyle will birth the child; my incarnate, predisposed to the use of drugs, alcohol or other negative behaviours to hide from the pain of an unfulfilling existence. Alternatively, he will utilize addictions to hide from the truth of his irrelevance or will spend a lifetime working to heal the emotional distresses and regrets from a sorrowful childhood. My right to a life of value far outweighs the defendants' desire to birth a child whose life will be of little or no value.

"On behalf of my incarnate and its future life I claim the right to choose loving, nurturing parents who are living fulfilling lives, able to teach unconditional love to their progeny. I petitioned the court to grant my request so I can contribute positive healthy emotional growth within the space/time Universe."

Soul Tobee sat, watching Solomon, searching his energy pattern for a reaction. Solomon's eyes had been closed for the latter half of Tobees' submission and remained closed for what seemed an eternity of non-existent time.

Eventually, Solomon looked up; "Thank you Soul Tobee; Court will take an imaginary 10-minute break to review evidentiary documents."

"Reporter Shaver here. There you have it. Plaintive Tobee has outlined his case to force the defendant to abort her pregnancy so it can have a more propitious birth. In previous testimony Tobee provided evidence that the Knebworths live a dysfunctional, self-abusive lifestyle and are therefore unfit to parent a child. He suggested if carried to term his future self will undoubtedly be similarly dysfunctional who will, in turn, produce additional dysfunctional children. A plaintiff-favourable decision here could affect major changes to the parental selection process.

The Defendant;

"All rise." The Bailiff barked. "Court is now in session."

Solomon assumed his place on the bench and turned to Mrs. Knebwort: "Madam; you may reply to the evidence presented by the plaintiff?

Advocate Cromwell stood: "Your Honourable One, we move this case be dismissed on the grounds that it is the Universal right of the female to have total, irrevocable dominion over her body. No speculative damages offered by the defendant can supersede the Universal law of " Eve Knebworth started to rise but it was her voice that rose; "I want my baby! And you can't take him away!

Solomon was quick to gavel with a crack of lightning and a rumble of thunder; "Order! Order! Your Advocate is speaking on your behalf and if you continue to interject I will remove your voice from the proceedings.

She muttered: "Yes honourableness." as she sat.

Advocate Cromwell continued: "In rebuttal to the plaintiffs' injunction, the defendant states she will accept whichever soul enters the unborn but declares the embryo is of her body and cannot be destroyed.

"My client would be deeply bereft at the loss of her baby causing further damage to a life already traumatized by an abusive, alcoholic family of origin and by a life of recreational drugs attempting to escape her. deep; aw, um, emotional; aw, um, wounds" Realizing her plea for sympathy because of childhood trauma, was describing the main argument of her opponent she hesitated...

Solomon waited… then gently coughed "Ahem."

Cromwell brightened; "Yes, your Honour. It is our position that a woman's body is sacrosanct to her decisions and no one can take away that right. Neither this court nor God herself can abrogate that right. We are complete.

Tobee stood, Solomon frowned; "Soul Tobee, you wish to add something?"

"Your Honour, the argument you just heard from Advocate Cromwell is precisely my argument for an order to abort the zygote at this stage. I do not wish to harm Mrs. Knebwort nor usurp her right to birth me but it is heartbreaking to see another precious life wasted on the trash heap of childhood trauma through toxic parenting. It is my right to have a happy and fulfilling life engendered by functional parenting able to raise children in an environment of unconditional love. I request the court to order my reassignment to an incarnation that will support my goal of sanity. I am complete."

Solomon spoke: "Thank you both for bringing this challenge to the court. As earth time is an important commodity concerning this matter, I will deliver my determination tomorrow." With a thump of the gavel, spoke; "Court is adjourned to an imaginary ten o'clock tomorrow."

"Morley Shaver here. You have just heard a soul petitioning for the right to be born into a healthy, loving environment. We have also heard from the defendant who claims the right of the inviolability of her body and that it is her intention to carry the fetus to term. Candles will burn late into the night as Justice Solomon wrestles with this judicial challenge.

The Verdict:

"All rise;" The High Court of Universal Justice is now in session; The All Compassionate Lord Solomon presiding.

Solomon entered slowly. He climbed the three steps to the bench and surveyed the courtroom. With rich resonate tones he began; "From the beginning of space-time, when creatures first saw themselves as separate individuals apart from the collective oneness of all, this problem of; 'my need supersedes your needs,' has plagued all beings. When souls incarnate into a human form they see themselves as separate individuals and only occasionally function in the highest good for the collective. But we are not here to reinvent the proper order of things but to resolve this one instance of an age-old question 'Does my right to act in my best interest take priority over your right to act in your best interest?'

"Both manifested and unmanifested beings appear to be missing the point. It is not important what one does in a carnate life but how much one takes away from the experiences they have chosen to have within their assigned lifetime. Remember, all of us choose to incarnate to bring positive and negative experiences to ourselves that are opportunities for spiritual growth; to become aware; to become conscious. Learning to love unconditionally is the true and only purpose of life.

"I will not interfere with the pregnancy. Nor will I abandon Mr. Tobees' request for a fulfilling life. I hereby obligate the Knebworth's to take steps to learn and become aware that child rearing is a great responsibility and need to look closely at the needs of the neonate. Find the potential within the child and nurture it. This is the only important responsibility you will have in your entire life. You are hereby directed to take steps to learn to nurture the infants' growth in a healthy, loving environment."

Looking towards Soul Tobee Solomon continued; "I obligate the plaintiff to be born as intended and to search and find a path of healing. Contained within life's wounds there are gifts and it is your responsibility to seek them out and in the healing of those gifts, you will find the fulfillment you seek. In so doing, the wounds of the Universe are also healed. Everyone's only task in life, and the reason we choose to incarnate, is to learn unconditional love, first for ourselves and then for others.

"I charge you both, the plaintiff and the defendant with the responsibility to engender unconditional love within the space-time continuum. That is your only and true reason for existing. Learn unconditional self love then peace will reign throughout existence. Court is adjourned!" With a slam of the gavel, His eminence rose and exited the courtroom to the sound of applause.

This is Morley Shaver live from The High Court of Universal Justice where Chief Justice Solomon has again demonstrated his profound wisdom by solving a real-life dichotomy. We hope you enjoyed today's program of news and views of the growing awareness within the evolution of the Universe. Join us again next time here at the 'Evolution Observer' where we report news and views on the evolution of the Universe.

The Scrubbing Woman

A Dramatization of a confirmed true story

She scrubbed the cheap linoleum floor without purpose or intention. It wasn't dirty she just scrubbed the floor and scrubbed and scrubbed and then she scrubbed some more. She scrubbed to save her sanity. There was an occasional pause when she would stare blankly at the floor while her mind listened to the voices and then she would dip her brush in the pail and scrub some more. It wasn't as if there had ever been dirt there at one time, it's just that scrubbing was something she knew how to do and as long as she could force herself to scrub, the beast in her mind was held at bay.

The rage behind a powerless terror was there ready to pounce and drive her over the edge into insanity. Everything was wrong. The farm was gone, the house, the barn, the horses; those beautiful matching Percherons that had won top honours at Brandon country fair almost seven years ago now. The bank had taken everything they could and now everything was gone. So she scrubbed and scrubbed and scrubbed while her three-year-old son watched.

Bobby watched. He watched from the corner of the room; the corner near the front door where the deep of winter lie just beyond. He didn't say anything he just watched her scrub. Even at three, he knew something was wrong. He could feel the fear but couldn't see the danger. It was something concealed and nameless; some unseen threat to this scrubbing woman on whom his life depended. Not understanding how this could be, he vaguely understood her life depended on having a floor to scrub. Silent, he watched her scrub the floor with water from a bucket to which her silent tears were added.

The intensity of the feelings caused him to find some distraction and look away but soon his eyes would return to watch the scrubbing woman.

She scrubbed. She didn't know what else to do to keep from letting the emotional pain overwhelm her. It wasn't the poverty, nor was it the war that raged in Europe that in a year or two would demand her eldest child as fodder for the war machine. How did her dream world become the nightmare of this reality?

Her husband, who had been a part of the dream come true, had been crushed by his failure to succeed at farming. He had taken on the responsibility for three years of nearly total drought and the lowest price on record for the meagre wheat crop that was produced. He took no notice of the hundreds of other farmers forced into bankruptcy by years of little to no rain, unsympathetic banks and an impotent government that offered little in the way of support. It was his fault, or so he believed, so to hide the shame of his failure, he found alcohol and the misery of fellow imbibers that shared his story with shame of their own.

She scrubbed and scrubbed the spot seeing dirt that may have existed only in her mind. She scrubbed to erase the wound that was almost too much to endure. Her shame was that she offered herself to him sexually wanting to feel loved, wanting to feel worthy and to extinguish the persistent belief that she was not. It was completely unintentional and unintended that she had become pregnant. This accidental child that had grown within her validated her belief, beaten into her in childhood, that she was a mistake; not worthy of being loved. That shame burned in her belly along with the growing foetus. Maybe it was post-partum depression or the loss of her dreams or the emotional abandonment of her mate or the combination of them all that drove her to want to escape into death.

Not wanting to keep remembering the pain of the last nine years, the bankruptcy, the fear, the shame, the fighting over the alcoholic episodes, she scrubbed. Nothing good existed in her life beyond this floor and this scrub brush, so she scrubbed and she cried.

Bobby watched her scrub. Although unaware of the source, he could feel the depth of her despair. He felt her sorrow but was unaware that this woman, who was his world, had come face to face with something that threatened her profoundly. He was also unaware that it was a profound threat to him as well.

It wasn't wisdom that described to him the danger of this situation; it was his natural animal instinct for survival that he responded to. His gestation was not as a wanted child conceived in love with sweet birds singing on the windowsill. Indeed, his time in utero along with the blood that brought him the nutrients from which he thrived, he was awash in the hormones of guilt, shame, fear. And the dark angry energy of the interchanges external to his amniotic environment were threats to him as well.

All were the vibrations from which he prepared to meet the world beyond. No; he did not think in material terms as he had no concept of the material world but he knew about energy and instinctively he knew which was a nurturing vibration was and which vibration represented danger.

She had already had her kids. She wanted no more. She had sought advice from her mother about the possibility of contacting an abortion doctor in Winnipeg but the advice she received was to never invest in regret, legal or not. And as he watched her scrub he had no awareness that this Mother couldn't abandon her child's survival. Neither of them were aware that her profound obligation to nurture the child would also keep her alive. The gift of her accidental pregnancy was to give her someone to love and a reason to live at an intensely bleak, loveless, time in her life.

For Bobby, the wound the newborn received through the circumstances of the pregnancy and birth provided the plotline from which he would write the story of his life. He would seek continually to change the belief that he was flawed in some concealed way, creating a purpose to exist in a senseless world.

However; there was still the threat of a nervous breakdown that might push her over the edge. This was the primary threat to Bobby's existence and the other threats; an alcoholic Father, a rageful brother whose mother's love he had stolen were all of lesser importance at the moment. This child was the reason his Mother would stay alive and stay sane but also just as true the circumstances of his conception and subsequent birth were a major contributor to the source of her pain.

So here were two people; a woman on her knees fighting to find the courage to stay sane and alive if only for the care and safety of this flesh she had generated and a child unaware of the psychological implications wanting reassurance that he was safe.

He had enough of silent watching and arose to walk to his Mother. With arms outstretched, he sought to be picked up. She understood that the child only wanted to be loved so she dropped the scrub brush in the bucket along with the unresolved traumas to pick Bobby up and hold him close.

Epilogue:

The scrubbing woman became the anonymous mom at the grocery store in a "just-plain-folks" neighbourhood and lived to be 90. The child having been born a lost child into a lost generation decided he would not die a lost adult and sought to live a life of adventure. That adventure continues.

The Million, Million, Million Stars

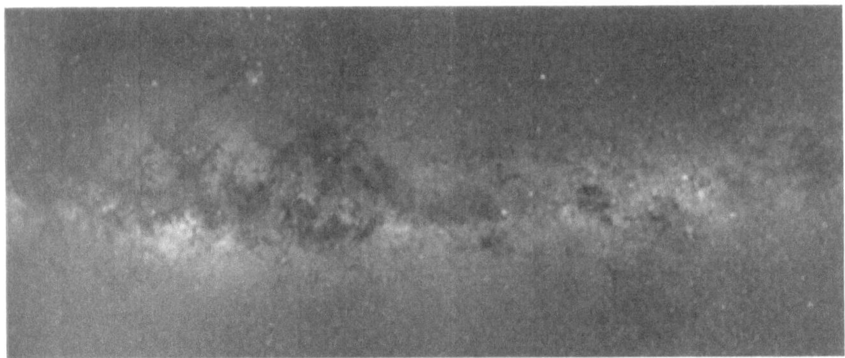

A True Story

It's Cold Out! Put a hat on!!

Do you know the Northern Ontario winter; the crisp, cold, crystal clear, Northern Ontario winter? Yes, the cold can be bitter, not to mention the icy chill added by the wind, and it can snow so hard one cannot see beyond a few feet, but in its kinder, gentler, white blanket, moments; it can be awe-inspiring in its beauty.

Picturesque scenes of snow-covered pine trees in a landscape of sheer beauty with an exhilarating freshness that demands one to come out and play. Yes, come out and play. After all, I was only five-and-a-half years old when we moved into the lumber camp. Camp Abitibi 220 was a lumber camp halfway up the west shore of Lake Nipigon about 180 miles, more or less due north of Thunder Bay. This is where we lived from the fall of 1945 until the spring following my ninth birthday.

My Father was the Stores Manager and he, along with the Camp Cook and the Woods Manager, was permitted to have their families with them. So, along with my Mother and one of my two older brothers, off we went to camp.

No little red schoolhouse

I was home-schooled in reading, writing and math but mostly I was allowed to explore and roam the camp at will. The lumber camp was the perfect teacher that suited the unquenchable curiosity of this young explorer. I learned how blacksmiths make and mount shoes on the dozen workhorses that were used to drag felled trees to the river. I learned how it is for the cooks and 'cookees' to feed 50 or so hungry men three meals a day cooked on wood-fired stoves.

From the fall of 1945, when we moved into the lumber camp until we left in the late spring of 1949, after my ninth birthday, the camp taught me about life, both its joys and its sorrows.

From the River.

The camp was situated overlooking the Poshkakogan River which was our source of fresh water. During the summer a hand pump was used to draw water from the river but in the winter, when the river was frozen and it was safe to take horses out onto the river, ice water was drawn from a hole chopped in the ice. Bucket by bucket the water was drawn and spilled into a huge, square, wooden tub that rested on a ski-equipped sled. After filling, the sled was then pulled up the hill to supply the water needs of the camp.

The day I learned about our winter water source was also the day I learned about fluid dynamics and never to hitch a ride on the back of a sled carrying a tub filled with ice cold water. The tub was taller than I, but at the back I was able to climb onto the sled, holding on at the top edge of the water-filled tub. As the sled started up the hill the equivalent of at least a full bucket of ice-cold water leaped from the back of the tub which then splashed over my face, mittened hands and down both inside and outside of my parka. Despite the sunny day at minus twenty-degree weather, my water-soaked parka and mittens began to freeze solid in a few short minutes. I was most grateful that my Mother and a warm cabin was only a short, stiff walk up the hill.

I Didn't Know Pigs could Swim.

At the far eastern end of the camp was a pig sty where several pigs were kept for fresh meat. One fall day a sow dropped 8 piglets. They were small enough to escape the confines of the sty and wander throughout the camp. Down from the main part of the camp at the river below was a narrow bridge. It was just boards nailed onto a log boom that floated right at the river level and in the fall the bridge caught lots and lots of fallen leaves as they drifted downstream. The warm afternoon sun would dry out the top layer of leaves which to the young piglets appeared to be dry land. They would step out unto the leaves and plop, down they would go. A few seconds later a little pig would pop back up; squealing loudly and paddling their way to shore. I remember laughing out loud at their antics.

A Horse with No Name.

Winter wasn't the only thing harsh in Northern Ontario. The reality is that life in the camp was harsh and at times dangerous work. The job of the cutters using hand saws and axes was to fell and trim the spruce and balsam and a few jackpine. The trees were cut into 16-foot lengths and then dragged onto the frozen river using horses. When the river ice broke in the spring the logs floated downriver, to be collected into large log booms and then to sawmills or paper mills.

One winter a horse fell through the ice resulting in a broken foreleg. There was no veterinarian; no economic sense to try to save it, so a horse with a broken leg was a dead horse. A rifle was brought to the river and the horse was killed. Then using a team of horses the unfortunate creature was dragged to an isolated area some distance away from the camp area and left for the wolves. Much of the carcass was gone within a week; a winter bonus for the wolves, foxes and other carrion eaters of the forest.

Bear, Bear

Fall in Northern Ontario, wrapped in glowing yellows, reds and sepias can be inspiringly beautiful. It was a radiant fall day and as I walked past the blacksmith barn I noticed the big doors were open and heard the clang, clang; ping, ping sound of the blacksmith working.

Beyond the horse stables, the hay barn, past the pigpen and some distance away was the camp garbage dump. One of my pleasures was using the tin cans I had positioned along the top edge of the dump as targets for my BB-gun. I hadn't even gotten as far as the spot where garbage was tipped into the dump when I took my first shot. The shot dmade a pinging sound as it bounced off of a can. I started to reload for another shot when seemingly from nowhere, the biggest black bear the world has ever seen, stood up!

Now the cardinal rule of woods lore is to never run away from an encounter with a bear. The brilliance of the bear mind is that anything that runs away must be food or it wouldn't be running away. I had yet to acquire that bit of wisdom so I ran! I ran as hard and fast as my eight-year-old legs would carry me! I flew past the pigpen, past the hay storage and into the barn looking for the safety of the blacksmith yelling; "Bear! Bear!"

The blacksmith was a huge man to begin with and armed with a forge hammer he could probably subdue a bear of any size, but by the time he got to the barn door, the bear was nowhere to be seen. From then on, my momentary island of refuge, the big, burly, Swedish blacksmith laughed and teased me relentlessly about hunting imaginary bears with a BB gun.

The Trapper

Old Joe was likely a Meitei or Cree, but no one ever spoke to me about his heritage. I didn't know he was any different from the Finns, Swedes, Ukrainians and other immigrants that made up the cutters. He was just Old Joe who ran a trap line along the river. He lived without shelter of any kind and once in a while come out of the bush to visit the camp. He was always welcomed to eat food from the mess hall and would sleep in the blacksmith's barn.

Joe taught me how to make a rabbit snare and how to make a snow shelter and told me that if you sleep outdoors in winter you will never freeze to death because the cold will always wake you up.

One day as he was washing up, he had me stick my finger in the pail of water beside him. He told me the importance of a person is measured by the size of the hole left when he pulled his finger out. I laughed and told him I was never going to leave a hole in the water.

At the time I thought he was just teasing me but years on I realized, my friend, the old native was a pseudo-Zen Master offering me a lesson about ego.

The Adventure Continues!

My years at Camp 220 were filled with adventure. In those years I learned many fascinating things about the world I lived in; however, there is one experience that has been a constant memory over the ensuing years.

It was in the winter of 1948/49 and I was not yet nine years old. With only one set of skis between of us, my brother and I and one of the younger cutters took turns skiing the hill beside our cabin down to the frozen river. I had just had my turn, so after dragging the skis back up the hill, I brushed the snow off of a pile of wood siding slats and lay down to wait my turn.

That far north dark comes early in winter so I had seen the night sky many times before but I don't remember having brought it into conscious attention. That night, for the first time, I became aware of what it was I was seeing.

In the unimpeded openness of a crystal clear Northern Ontario winters night, the sky was ablaze with stars displaying vastness beyond vastness, immensity beyond immensity. A shock of realization ran through me. I had no words for the sense of awe I was feeling and no place to put the awareness of the immensity of the starlit sky. This was the truth; we humans are minuscule in this vastness.

I was nearly nine years old looking up at uncountable dots of silver. Countless tiny lights tinged with hints of blues and reds floating on a sea of blackness. Awestruck by the magnificence of the sky I was totally humbled by the sight of the heavens above me.

There were a million, million, million stars and I felt a sense of wonder to see this vastness beyond vastness. Life's mundane, day to day drama had been drawn back for a moment and behind the curtain was the truth that as conscious beings we are living an amazing adventure that we are allowed to recognize and appreciate the wonder of this Universe that we inhabit.

My limited knowledge of the millions dead from the recent second world war had made me aware of life's transient nature and in this immensity of time and space, the realization that I am less than minuscule was not going to ensure my survival. I concluded this might be a good time to ask. "Please God; I want to live to be very old." My almost nine-year-old thinking saw the time from then to the year 2000 seemed forever away so I asked; "I want to live to the year 2000." I am sincerely gratefully that request was granted and thankfully that request has been renewed annually, one year at a time.

The gift given me at that moment of realizing the immensity of the Universe was a desire to see behind the curtain again; to know and understand the truth of the Universe. That has been my life's journey. Perhaps this is what all humans seek, each in our own way; to know and understand the meaning of this vast puzzle we call the Universe. If we survive; and I believe we will, we will eventually solve the mystery behind the creation of the million, million, million stars.

Angelic Stranger

Both he and his horse were dust-covered as though they had come from some distant place and had been travelling for days, maybe weeks. In the bright midday sunshine, every villager noted the stranger clad in black with suspicion. Black shirt, black pants, black Stetson and he sat atop a big, black mount. He rode slowly down the dusty main street looking for the livery stables to board his horse and at the end of main street, he found his quest. He dismounted and led his mount through the open doors into the cool dark of the barn.

A young boy took the reins of the horse and said: "Howdy stranger, looks like you've been on a mighty long journey; where you from?" Not replying, the stranger reached into a pocket of his vest and handed the boy a small gold coin. "Take good care of him," He said, and turned to walk back into the light.

He had noted the location of the saloon down the street and took to the shaded side until he was opposite, then he crossed the street. Pausing at the top of the veranda steps to notice a chair at the very end of the porch, he entered the saloon and waited just inside the doorway to become accustomed to the darkened interior. Seeking out the bar he found a spot and ordered a whiskey. Again from his vest pocket he produced a small gold coin and gesturing to the bottle he said; "Leave it." and drank the sour liquid from the shot glass in one quick gesture.

Most in the bar had noticed the low slug holster holding the Colt Frontier revolver and assumed the stranger was some kind of gunfighter. Our stranger picked up the whiskey bottle and headed for the open doorway. The bartender cleared his throat to speak; "Sheriff don't like …" but thought better of finishing the words out loud he spoke softlly to himself; 'whiskey on the street', and went back to wiping the bar with a somewhat less than clean towel.

Stepping beyond the doorway our stranger turned and walked to the chair and sat down. He poured a shot into the glass he had emptied at the bar and set the whiskey bottle on the floor beside the chair. Unlike his previous drink he sipped from the glass; put his boots up on the veranda railing and leaned the chair back towards the wall.

The delegation of the barber, the general store owner and the feed store manager were the first to arrive at the sheriff's office. "What are you going to do about this killer in our midst? They demanded. "What killer," the sheriff asked. "What makes you think he is a killer? He's just a stranger and long as he follows the laws or we know better about him, he's just another drifter on his way to somewhere else."

"Just wait 'till McGruder hears about this you'll be looking for a new job." McGruder who owned the biggest ranch this side of Abilene, employed most of the local population which meant he was the controlling, self-serving, politico of the territory.

Right now that was the least of Sheriff Toby's problems. No one liked having a stranger in town and especially one that looked like he might be a gunfighter. Even so, the stranger had not broken any law, nor had he done anything to disrupt the calm and peace of Sheriff Toby's little town. The stranger was just having a quiet drink by himself on the veranda of the saloon and the Sheriff noted he had not taken his whiskey off the premises. The Sheriff pondered the thought that he should at least go and ask a few questions. "To what end?" He asked and sat down.

By late afternoon with much of the whiskey was still left in the bottle, the stranger remained motionless; feet against the railing; faced mostly covered by the brim of his hat as though he was napping in the afternoon sun. Sheriff Toby watched and waited.

The saloon owner, Rubin came out to the front entrance with the lit lantern he always hung at dusk. The sheriff noted that even though the sun was just beginning to set, it was a bit early for the lantern but he assumed Rubin was looking for an excuse to check that the stranger was still there.

The nightmare Sheriff Toby feared began to unfold. McGruder's hot-headed young 18-year-old son, Ralph, was dismounting at the hitching post just outside the Sheriff's office and as he did; he removed a double-barrelled shotgun from his saddle scabbard. Ralph immediately turned and headed across the street; confronting the stranger as he did; "Hey gunfighter. You lookin' for trouble? Well, you shor'nuff found it?" He raised the shotgun to his shoulder and as he stepped forward he yelled; "You're not welcome here so draw that gun or leave!" The gunfighter didn't move but the Sheriff sure did. At a full run, he was out the door leapt off the boardwalk gun in hand and within three strides was directly behind Ralph. Grabbing his weapon by the gun barrel he whipped the handle with full force into the back of Ralph's head. Just as the Sheriff's blow made contact with Ralph's head the shotgun veered slightly to the left and exploded with both barrels unloading a hail of pellets at the saloon front.

At ten paces a shotgun blast is deadly and the pellets penetrated the saloon window killing the cattle herder sitting with his back to the glass. The spread of the pellets also blasted through the open doorway wounding several cowboys imbibing at the bar. It also blew apart the glass bottom of the lantern that hung near the doorway. The flame of the lantern followed the cascading liquid from the broken reservoir spilling the contents into the doorway that immediately erupted into flames. Whether it was the shotgun blast or the stranger that had knocked over the whiskey bottle spilling its contents and adding to the inferno was not known but within seconds the tinder-dry front of the building was ablaze.

Upon hearing yells of; "Fire! Fire!" the local working girls and their visitors to the upstairs rooms scrambled out onto the roof of the veranda in various states of undress while tongues of flames began to curl over the edge of the roof.

In the ensuing chaos that followed the stranger rose from his chair walked calmly through the flames pausing briefly at the doorway to look at the pandemonium of flames and the bleeding wounded inside the saloon. Untouched by the fire, he calmly turned and stepped down the few steps to the dusty street and started walking towards the livery stables.

Sherrif Toby was distracted attending to the unconscious Ralph and by the general chaos of the unfolding events, he didn't notice the central character of the unfolding horror was headed to the stables and his horse. When Sheriff Toby saw the flames licking at the empty chair he guessed that the visitor was leaving and headed towards the horse barn.

The stranger emerged from the stables riding his big, black stallion.

"Stranger, hold up; I have some questions I would ask."

"Why is that Sheriff? You already know as much as I do and my job here is done."

"What job? What's your name?"

As the stranger pulled alongside the Sheriff, he leaned over and spoke softly.

"My friends call me Dando which means giver, and my full name is; Angel Dando Muerte." The stranger dressed in black then spurred the flanks of his big, black horse, but instead of breaking into a gallop; both he and his rider simply vanished.

Sheriff Toby's dropped to his knees. "Dando Muerte, The Angel of Death. Dear God save us! Save us all!"

Bluebonnets Grow Wild in Texas

Bluebonnets danced around Julie Davis's white, sleeveless dress as she walked the sunlit field near the paddock where her horses grazed. She loved that bluebonnets grew wild in abundance in Texas. With a lot on her mind, she gathered a small bouquet for her vase. Perhaps a little beauty would soothe her unease about tonight's meeting.

There was always tension meeting with the Crawfords. Yes, they were her neighbours but they were also competing racehorse breeders. Perhaps enough time had passed so they understood there was nothing she could have done to change what happened. Not since Gallant Fox and Citation, both Kentucky Derby winners had there been such controversy about drugging.

It had been four years since Crawford's horse; Multitasker had been disqualified for showing positive for performance-enhancing drugs.

This left Julie's horse, MoonRocket, in second place to collect the top prize.

The Kentucky Derby is a 1 1/4 mile race for three-year-old thoroughbred horses at Churchill Downs in Louisville, Kentucky. Bill and Emma Jean Crawford were the owners of the horse, Multitasker that had been the winner of the majority share of the 3.4 million dollar prize money at the 140th running of the Kentucky Derby horserace known as the 'Run for the Roses.'

The winner that is; for 20 minutes until a blood test showed the banned substance Etorphine. Etorphine, also called "elephant juice," because of its use on large animals, was a dangerous stimulant used to numb pain and prep a horse to run its best. Julie's horse, MoonRocket, the second-place winner, was awarded the money.

Bill Crawford was one of the two top breeders in Texas, the other being Bluebonnet Farms owned by Arnold and Julie Davis. They were meeting today to discuss how they could cooperate to breed a guaranteed Derby winner. Julie also wanted to tell the Crawfords she had hired Roscoe Tanner, Crawfords and Multitasker's disgraced trainer who had been banned 4 years ago for doping.

Julie could feel her anxiety rising as she watched a Cadillac driving along the road to the farm. The hood ornament made of the longhorns of Texas cattle identified the car as Crawford's. "Hello Bill; welcome to Bluebonnet Farms," Julie called out as she walked to greet her visitors. "Hello, Emma Jean. I'm so glad you and Bill agreed to this meeting. It's been too long; after all, we are neighbours."

Exiting from his car, Bill gave an unsmiling reply: "Well Julie, I only agreed to this to keep Emma Jean happy and hopefully gain some of the money back you stole from me four years ago. "Hello, Julie." Emma Jean spoke as she gave Julie a perfunctory hug.

The trio entered the house and was about to be greeted by Julie's husband Arnold when Bill yelled out; "What in hell is he doing here?" Bill was referring to Roscoe Tanner who was seated on the leather divan next to the flagstone fireplace. "Come on Emma Jean, we're leaving."

"Wait, Bill, please don't rush away. Roscoe is the best horse trainer in Texas and his ban has been lifted. Besides, it was never proved that he drugged your horse!"

"This scummy low life, cost me over a million dollars in prize money, possibly millions in stud fees, and he cost me the shame of running a drugged horse." Pointing a finger at Roscoe; "You lying scumbag, I shoulda killed you the day of the race." Turning on his heel he stormed towards the door; "Emma Jean!", he yelled then turned and added; "I tell you right now, next week's Breeders Cup is mine. Tumbleweeds' gonna win me the 5 million dollar prize money."

Because of preps and chores; Julie and Arnold didn't arrive at the Breeders Cup until late Friday. They had entered MoonRocket's offspring, MoonRaker to race tomorrow. "Arnold sweetheart, go get me a blanket, I'm going to stay here the night to make sure MoonRaker is safe. I'll see you at breakfast."

It was a dark of the moon night and a feeling of anxiety stalked the darkened alleyways. Nothing moved, no throat rattles from the horses, no dogs barked, only an edgy feeling permeated the stables. The gate to Tumbleweeds stable didn't make a sound as it was opened and a hooded figure silently moved inside, leaving the gate ajar.

A voice cried out "Now!" and in an instant, the stable lights flashed on to reveal, Julie Davis, standing there frozen, a large syringe in her hand, oozing an occasional droplet of liquid from the tip of its needle. Slowly her face reddened, her mouth contorted and she began to emit a mournful scream; "Ayyeeeee!" She raised the syringe over her head, turned and began a lunge toward Bill Crawford. Bill grabbed Julie's arm and smashed it down against the stall gate. He smashed it down again hard and the syringe fell to the ground. The struggle was over quickly and Julie fell to the straw-covered floor crying.

It only took half an hour for the police to arrive and arrest Julie for several crimes. She was cuffed and as she was being placed in the back of the police car, she was overheard saying to the Officer; "Do you like bluebonnets? I love bluebonnets. Do you know bluebonnets grow wild in Texas?"

Jane of the Car

Their trips to the drive-in movie theatre were always the same. Frank would fall asleep and Jane would quietly leave the vehicle to go to the concession stand; get popcorn, Milk Duds, and a soda then return to the car to watch the movie.

As Jane walked back to the car with her goodies, the car-side speakers suddenly went silent and the screen went black, throwing the entire lot into darkness. She stopped, temporarily blinded. Then, the screen lit back up again, showing a visual of herself standing there holding popcorn, Milk duds and a soda. It was a perfect portrait of herself, Jane Ridley, on a screen 40 feet wide and 30 feet high.

It seemed as though everything had frozen; no sound, nothing moved. There was no light from the concession stand, no crickets chirped; she just stood there looking up at herself on a drive-in movie screen. Her mind desperately trying to figure out what was going on; Jane continued on a few feet and as she did the Jane on the screen continued on a few feet. She stopped again and looked up at the screen. Her mind raced. "Is this some kind of joke? She asked; "Well it isn't funny;" she said out loud.

"Hello Jane;" a voice said and paused, waiting for a response;

"Who are you? "How are you doing this?

You're doing this Jane. Well actually, your subconscious mind is doing this. She has taken control of everything around you and wants your attention. I'm your subconscious and I was watching your life unfold and you kept telling her how deeply dissatisfied you were with your life so it; she, your subconscious, decided to show you so that you can see your unhappiness yourself without distraction.

Our subconscious decided you weren't paying close enough attention to your life so everywhere you go wherever there is a screen you will be on it. Your subconscious will broadcast every moment of your life for you. Everything you do will be on a screen that only you can see but that is all you will ever see and the soundtrack will be your thoughts. A sort of mindfulness intensified.

"This is insane," Jane thought, which was spoken aloud by the character on the screen. The Jane of the screen spoke out loud the words as Jane, now sitting in the car thought them. "Have I gone insane; oh Gawd please don't let this happen;" Jane and the image on the screen spoke at the same time.

Because of the size and shape of the drive-in lot, there was a slight echo so that Jane of the car could hear Jane of the screen speak the words out loud as she thought them.

"Stop this, stop this! I can't hear myself talk and think at the same time."

"Of course, you can Jane; you do it all the time. You allow your mind to ramble on incessantly while your subconscious tries to keep up to the constant stream of mind chatter not connected at all to the awareness of the feelings offered up by the subconscious."

"That's not true;" she said. "I don't ramble on,… do I?"

The Jane of the screen looked directly at the Jane of the car; "We wouldn't talk to our best friend like that but your mind just reminded you of the accusation that we talk too much." Your mind is not your friend and we recognize this is a familiar accusation. After one of our rants or babble on lectures that we usually know little about. Don't we often hear the accusation; 'motor-mouth' and feel a sense of shame that we always talked too much. When and how often did our Mother tell us we talked too much and call us a 'chatterbox'?" asked the screen. And this is only one of a thousand childhood beliefs that no longer serve us.

This has got to stop or it will drive me insane; thought Jane and heard the words in the echo from the screen.

"We are already insane;" came the thought. "Being terrible unhappy and doing nothing to change it. That's insane;" came the words. "I believe in the common vernacular it is described as 'doing the same things over and over again and expecting different results."

"I have no idea where to start. I wouldn't even know where to begin;" spoke Jane of the car.

"Just create an intention to change and the Universe will bring us a way, a place to begin and a path. Just create the intention and mountains will move."

"It is time to take action. Pay attention to our feelings and our subconscious will open the doorway to a happy life of value. Wait and the subconscious part of us will atrophy and produce the chemicals to numb out our existence. Act now and our subconscious will inspire us to achieve the change we so desperately desire. Use the power of that desperation and our life will open a doorway to love and joy."

The screen flickered and went dark. It was dark for what seemed to Jane like it was forever. The concession lights came on and a voice came over the side speaker; "Sorry about the power failure. We have no idea what happened but we've fixed it and we will return to the movie; 'A beautiful mind' in just a moment. Enjoy.

The Alien

She squinted at the dark yellow leaves blowing in through the broken window, scattering to the corners of the room. She'd never had any friends and she had her translucent pink-tinged skin and pink-rimmed eyes to thank for that. Having never attended regular school didn't help her social status, either. Yet, on this freezing, cold night, she found herself huddled on the floor of an abandoned hunting shack, surrounded by girls she'd passed on the trail in the nearby woods. She startled when the red-headed one of them leaned towards her and spat out the words, "Truth or Dare?!"

Aylia could never get used to the aggressive nature of these earth people; "What is 'truth or dare' please?" she asked?

"Stupid alien,, its a…;" she paused, "Oh forget it, but we've got to do something to warm up or we'll freeze to death."

Aylia insisted; "No, please if this is common knowledge I should be learned of, please. Tell me, please."

"It's a game where you must choose to either tell the truth or do something weird that you really don't want to do.

I am always tell truth, why would I not please? The red-headed girl, frustrated at the innocence of the alien, either feigned or real. "Damn you girl; or whatever you are. I want to know. Are you a girl? Do you have all the right parts? Are you made the same as us girls?" She asked, gesturing at the others.

"I do not know please. When I arrived your medical staff declared me a girl and entered that information on my papers, but never having been introduced to why the doctors made that determination it is information I do not have as yet please."

"Well," Aylia's red-headed, protagonist stood up; "perhaps it's time we told you how and why they made that determination."

Just then a small device in Aylia's pocket made a sound. She took a small square box out of an unseen pocket and placed it to the side of her head. "Yes, please. Yes, there are three. Yes, I think good specimens of teenage females. Yes please, now would be a good time, thank you please."

"Well friends, you have been invited to meet my commander onboard our Mother ship. I hope it will be an eventful experience for all of you. Aylia turned to the red-headed girl. "I think I am going to particularly enjoy dissecting you, please; especially you please."

She spoke to the small square box; "Four to transport, please."

Dark yellow leaves continued blowing in through the broken window and scattering to the corners of the now-empty abandoned hunting shack.

The TreeHouse

The three were devoted friends; closer than brothers. Not genetically related but they shared a spirit of adventure. Today they were going to continue building the fort using boughs and branches brought down by the wind and rain of the storm in the past several days. Tommy had run ahead and yelled back to Sid and Joey; "You guys aren't going to believe this!!" There's a treehouse in our climbing tree.

It took only a minute of inspection before Tom began climbing the oak, with Sid right behind him. They easily reached the treehouse and discovered a rope ladder to drop for Joey.

Joey displayed his reluctance, pushing the ladder away; "I don't like this," he said; "This is too weird!" We were here just a week ago. Nobody can build a treehouse like this in a week. From the balcony, his two friends called out; Chicken! Chicken! Cluck, cluck!" With this challenge, Joey reluctantly climbed the ladder to follow his friends into the treehouse.

The interior lighting blinked. It flickered so fast it was hardly noticeable but something shifted and the door they had just entered disappeared along with windows and in their place down a corridor were six doors; each one with a small gold plaque marked 'Escape'.

"Now, what have we got ourselves into?;" "I'm scared!" said Sid, seriously scared!" A tremor in his voice confirming this. Joey spoke:" I told you guys this can't be real! Where is the door we just came in?" "OK! Ok! Let's just calm down;" said Tommy. One of these doors has got to lead us out of here.

The first door was labelled 'Escape', and under that were the words; 'Eat your way out.' Sid, whose nickname was 'Foodorator' because of his unsophisticated eating habits, spoke out. "Hey! This can't be all bad," he said as he opened the door. In front of him lay a table of hot pizza, pitchers of iced cola, with burgers and baskets of yam fries. Sid began to move towards the food but Joey grabbed his collar from behind and yanked him back. Don't be a dumb ass! This can't be real.

Sid, feigning injury, responded; "Yea, it sure looked real; even smelled real. Sid released the door handle and the door quietly closed. The trio moved on to the next door and read the label. 'Escape' followed by 'on wheels' Sid often dreamed of the day when he would own a four-stroke Yamaha dirt bike or perhaps a 250 cc Kawasaki. You can imagine the elation he felt when both of these machines appeared in the room before him. Sid moved into the room. Pleading voices called out; "Sid, wait! I don't trust this place!" Sid reached out and touched the Kawasaki, Nothing happened. The bike appeared to be real. The door remained open and both Joey and Tommy stood in the doorway watching. Sid grabbed the handlebars and leaned forward intending to mount the bike. As he did the door began to close. Joey and Tommy tried to hold it open but the closer Sid got to mounting the bike the more the door closed, "Sid. Wait don't"…. The motion to throw his leg over the stern of the bike didn't stop and with a hard slam, the door closed. There was silence as the boys tried to engage the latch which hung loose.

"What are we going to do?" From the other side of the door came the noise of a dirt bike engine. It roared a few times and then seemed to motor away from the tree house diminishing continually until it disappeared. Joey and Tommy looked at each other. Could it be? Sid actually escaped on a motorbike?

Moving to the next door, Tommy opened 'Escape; Sail away'. What appeared before Tommy was the deck of a large sailboat in heavy seas with waves breaking over the prow and sea spray blowing back through the open doorway. Dripping seawater, Tommy slammed the door shut. "That was insane. I love sailing but get seasick so no good in a storm.

The next door was labelled 'Escape; NASA's final frontier" At home, Joey's room was filled with model rockets, NASA memorabilia and photos of shuttle crews. He couldn't resist opening this door. What appeared was a lunar landscape, the lower half of the lunar lander from 1967, imprints of footsteps and a sun-bleached US flag. Ignoring the lack of air on the moon Joey stepped forward and as he did a fully functioning, pressurized space suit manifested about his body as the door closed behind him.

Tommy tried the 'final frontier' door latch again but to no avail. He moved to the last door which read; 'Escape: To nowhere in particular.' When he opened the door he saw the Oak he had climbed to get into the treehouse; a few scattered boughs and branches and last week's attempt at fort building. Tommy decided this was his escape route with a drop of 10 to 15 feet. He hung from the opening for few seconds and as he let go; the forested scene and Oak dissolved into a mist that wrapped around him in what seemed to be an endless fall, fading to black.

CNN Breaking News; Hundreds have been searching for the three missing boys whose bodies were found today in Roberts creek, swollen by recent rains.

A Snow Day

Goat Island, Niagara Falls, New York

There had been morning frost here in the Boston area and reports of continual snow falling in upstate New York with the temperature steadily dropping for a week.

As an environmental Professor, I was called to a meeting at the University Environmental Center regarding a serious problem at Niagara Falls. An American university had collaborated with a Canadian University to develop a machine that could control the weather. Something had gone wrong with the equipment and it appeared the machine was creating a new ice age using the power and the water of Niagara Falls.

The American and Bridal Veil Falls on the US side and the Horseshoe Falls on the Canadian side collectively drop over 750,000 gallons of water every second or 45million gallons of water per minute, most of which was being converted into freezing rain which cooled the atmosphere and then began falling as snow. Already a foot of snow has fallen in the northeastern states causing serious problems in upstate New York, into Vermont, New Hampshire and Maine.

We assumed that Dr. Smarkgrass, the inventor, was killed when the machine exploded, and likewise, the staff must have frozen to death so there was no one there who knew how to shut the machine down. I had that information locked in a small box sent to my office more than a month ago. The key to open the box was in the professor's office at the Niagara facility so someone had to take the box to Niagara, open it and turn the machine off. I was the only one with a 4 wheel drive vehicle with snow tires, so I prepared to go. By the time I headed west on Interstate 90 heavy snow was falling.

The news media had found out about the threat of an out-of-control deep freeze and panic set in. As I travelled westward, I passed thousands of vehicles that crawled, eastward, bumper to bumper through the deepening snow looking for a route south to escape the deepening freeze. Some had skidded off the roadway and were stuck in the snow unable to get back onto the highway. Those people might freeze to death in the growing cold but I dare not stop to help. I continued heading west into the snowstorm.

Fear grew in my chest as I glanced at the small box on the seat beside me and realized the importance of my mission. I said out loud; "I can do this." Snow-covered mile after snow-covered mile I drove into the snowstorm. Even with my 4 wheel drive and winter tires, I was very concerned wouldn't make it to Niagara before the roads became impassable.

Near Rochester, I was overjoyed to see a truck stop and prayed they were open and could pump fuel. I pulled in and started fueling before going inside to get some hot coffee.

"Where in blazes did you come from?" The attendant asked? "Boston, I replied and I've got to get to Niagara Falls."

"You're out of luck," he said. "The Interstate is closed and is gonna stay closed until this storm blows over. This is the worst one I've ever seen."

"Well, it isn't ever gonna' blow over unless I get to Niagara Falls," I replied

'If you can get past the barricade and get back onto I 90, then at 290 go north to the falls but I think you're crazy to try it."

Skirting the flashing lights of the barricade I continued west. As I got closer to my destination I avoided several cars stalled right on the highway unable to move through the deep snow.

The machinery was located in a building belonging to Friendship University on Goat Island situated between the two waterfalls. I drove across a narrow snow-covered bridge over water rushing to the edge of the falls. In the growing darkness, loomed a dark grey stone structure draped in snow and icicles. No light shone from the windows and the building was surrounded by a mist rising from the falls along with the falling snow giving the building a feeling of abandonment.

I pulled right up to the front steps. Leaving my headlights on, exited the car taking the box and a flashlight with me.

The front door was unlocked and partially open. I stepped inside to hear the screaming noise of a machine converting half a million gallons of water per second into a frozen vapour that was thrown into the air to come down as snow, snow and more snow continually adding to the new ice age.

"Where is Dr. Professor's office?" I asked of a frozen body perched over a computer desk. I continued; "In the far corner to the left. Thank you." Using my flashlight I made my way to a locked door in the corner office. I used the flashlight to smash the glass, reached in to release the lock and entered.

A grey-haired man in a tweed jacket lay face down on the floor so I knew this was the Professors office. I went to the desk and opened the top right-hand drawer. I quickly took the key that lay there and opened the box I removed a sealed envelope and hastily tore it open. In large capital letters was a message. ON THE CONTROL PANEL IN THE UPPER LEFT QUADRANT TURN THE POWER SWITCH TO OFF.

Camping Can Be Fun

Camping Can Be Fun

The campers on the site next to them were noisy, rude and downright obnoxious. She winced as more profanity echoed through the woods. Her husband Bob had insisted that camping would be 'educational and wholesome fun for the kids. Roger was age 8 and Susan was age 10. "Bob had sure gotten the educational part right;" She muttered to herself.

It was quite late when the fight their noisy neighbours were having finally quieted down. The following morning while they were cooking bacon and eggs, Bob and Helena decided to pack up and move to a different campground. They started to pull the tent pegs when their noisy neighbours walked into their campsite. "Hi were your noisy neighbours; Tim and Judy, and we've come over to apologize for the ruckus last evening. We finally asked my rather boisterous bad-mouthed cousin to leave and let us enjoy the quiet of this beautiful spot. I see you've begun to close up your camp but I invite you to stay. It's such a beautiful location. The forest, the lake and that cute little bridge at the entrance. It's a perfect location for a quiet rest up.

Both the children shouted; Yea! yea! stay, stay! With the promise of a more civilized noise level, it was decided they would stay. The noisy neighbours stayed to chat a while but the wind and darkening clouds foretold a storm was brewing and they returned to their campsite.

Even though Roger was not an accomplished swimmer, he and Jenny went to the beach to wade and look for seashells. It wasn't long before they came running back; Yelling; Bear! Bear! Sure enough, they were followed by a huge black Bear lured by the smell of food the bear came into the campsite and went directly to use his powerful paws to smash open the cooler to eat hot dogs, all the eggs and half the potato salad. Everyone had retreated to the car to watch the bear either eat or destroy all the remaining food and then rip open their tent looking for more only to leave a pile of animal droppings in gratitude for the food.

The family emerged from the car to begin to clean up the campsite but the darkened sky fulfilled its promise and the rain began. It wasn't long before the rain turned into a torrent of rain mixed with hail. The wind picked up and began to toss anything that was not nailed down into an airborne missile of some sort. Eventually, the wind became so strong a small tornado was spawned that ripped through the park picking up picnic tables and exposed camping gear and hurling them against cars and tents as the family huddled in their car covered with the sleeping bags and pillows in an attempt to keep warm from the rapidly cooling temperature. The 90 mph wind caught the tent awning lifting the whole tent and dragging it a few feet before ripping the awning completely away from the main body of the tent. The tornado ripped open the part of the tent where

Roger had left his beloved stuffed teddy bear and before he could be stopped he jumped from the car to save his toy bear. The wind quickly wrapped Roger in the tent awning and hurled him high in the air and out over the lake before letting him fall into the water. As the tornado moved further down the lake the neighbour Tim who had been out inspecting damage heard the cries for help from Roger out in the lake. Tim, an Olympic champion swimmer, made a headlong dive into the water to save Roger from drowning and return him to his parents

While the drenching rain had extinguished most of the campfires the strong wind had fanned the flames of a few of the barbecues and pit fires, blowing burning charcoal and embers into the nearby brush, igniting the underbrush and setting the surrounding forest ablaze. As the flames grew Bob hurried everyone into the car and rapidly drove to the exit which was just beyond the small bridge that was no longer there. It had been washed away in the flood which had followed the torrent of rain and hail. He slammed on the brakes to avoid plunging into the rushing waters

Trying to cross the raging creek meant certain death by drowning and a full-on forest fire was inching ever closer from behind them; not to mention a huge hungry black bear somewhere on the loose, giving them little hope of escaping imminent death

Suddenly the car was surrounded by an intensely bright light and a buzzing sound filled the car. One by one the four people disappeared starting with the children and then Helena followed by Bob. By itself, the car shifted into gear and plunged into the overflowing river. The unidentified saucer-shaped object which had been hovering over the stopped car then manoeuvered out over the lake and rapidly rose upwards to disappear among the remnant storm clouds with their four new humanoid specimens; two adults and two children.

Just Clowning Around

Twinkling lights that hung in the window blinked on and off, inviting the passers-by to come into the coffee shop and out of the freezing rain. She chose a spot where she could watch the people coming and going. She wondered; "What will he look like? Or could it be a she?" Without a description, the information that this place was going to be robbed this evening was nearly useless.

The bell on the door kept chiming and her neck was getting sore from looking up to assess who came in or notice who left, all the while, wondering what the thief was going to look like.

She nervously tapped the rim of her cup, making a clicking sound, while beneath her coat she fingered her VPD badge. Officer Tammy Steele had recently joined the downtown core beat and quickly gained the trust of the homeless, crack-heads and druggies by treating them with a little respect. Gladdis, the marijuana seller, wanting to buy a little safety from being busted; became her informant. "Should I trust her?;" Tammy questioned.

Near 8 pm, a slim grubby-looking character in a hoodie entered who attracted the attention of Officer Steele. The hood was drawn foreward to cover his head which then hid most of his face from view. "This has got to be our thief," Officer Steel thought to herself, as she tensed her body to raise and deal with whatever was next. His hand dove into the pouch of his hoodie and withdrew a few coins to count them. He then walked to a nearby table with his hand out seeking enough to buy a coffee. "OK, so it's not him.

At near 8:30 a very short person walked in the door. A dwarf dressed in a clown's costume with a cherry red wig and a tiny red hat perched atop his head. He wore a clown mask with a comedic red nose covering the lower half of his face. His clothing was carnival-like with each quadrant a different colour and he carried a tin clown-horn.

"How unusual to see a clown in a coffee shop." Officer Steel thought to herself. The miniature-sized clown surveyed the room, then walked over to a table and sat down.

Within minutes a second dwarf entered dressed as a Harlequin clown with a full black and white chequered costume, matching tam and shoes. A black mask covered the upper half of his face in traditional Harlequin style and he joined the seated dwarf.

Officer Steele satisfied herself her thief had yet to arrive and went back to door surveillance.

Shortly a third Dwarf entered, This one wore an oversized pink shirt that had bright red ruff at the neck and wrists. His light blue, stovepipe pants were oversized to match his shirt and he wore clownlike whiteface paint with exaggerated red-painted lips and red nose. He also wore a bright yellow hat with green polka dots.

Clown three was followed by dwarf four dressed identically except for a bright green hat with yellow polka dots. These two also sat at the corner table

All at once the clowns stood and brandished bear spray dispensers.

The first clown to enter spoke out loud: "So you just might ask who in hell are we, Were the badass gang, the Gang of Three. So just stay calm and don't get funny. Cause we're just here to take your money."

The Harlequin Clown complained, "But we agreed, we're the Gang of four!.The number one clown spoke again "Oh shut up Numbers! Two, take and empty the cash drawer. Three, get the Barista to open the safe in the office." If he won't do it give him a shot of bear spray till he does

Officer Steele, stood brandishing her badge in one hand and her gun in the other. She yelled out "Vancouver PD; you are all under arrest for robbery.

Clown One called out; "Group Plan 'B' and the clowns immediately stopped what they were doing and surrounded her with Harlequin behind her getting down on all fours. Clown One approached her with hands outstretched. "Do you want to put the cuffs on me officer? Before she could respond, Clown One rammed into her pushing her backwards. With Harlequin behind her, Officer Steele fell, landing flat on her back, and striking her head hard against the floor.

The two clowns at her sides immobilized her hands while One and Harlequin started searching through her coat and purse for handcuffs. Her gun was thrown over the counter. Just then the hoodie, whom Officer Steele had incorrectly identified as the thief stood pulling a badge from the pocket. and yelled; "Vancouver PD: You are all under arrest!"

Clown One yelled "Group Plan 'C" and all four clowns headed on the run for the door. With Clowns one two and three escaping by pushing Hoodie out of the way and over a table. Unfortunately for Harlequin, he was the last one to head for the door. Hoodie tackled him as he tried to escape and Offficer Steele who had quickly recovered placed the checkered Harlequin in hand cuffs.

Steele spoke to Hoodie. " I don't recognize you. who are you? I'm officer, Joe Virtoli an undercover cop who just happened to be here. I'm sure our Harlequin friend here will lead us to his friends in the gang of three.

Trick or Treat

A strong, biting wind whistled through the branches making the rustling sound of dry leaves and along with the darkening skies that set the mood. The mansion, said to be the home of a magician, with its peeling paint appeared abandoned but light in the windows each night said otherwise.

Street lamps lit the way as children hurried past the magician's house with their Halloween booty bags but no one dared venture up the path to knock on the door of this house.

Inside the magician stood in front of a huge stone fireplace in which sat an equally large cauldron over a fire. It was Annwn, the magical caldron from the Otherworld that he had managed to acquire by trick and treachery from an antique dealer in Wales, England.

'I am Merlyn,' began the incantation, 'and I command the sweat of ten thousand archers to coalesce into the stone of the legendary King Arthur' embedded in which is Arthur's jeweled sword.

All of the candles throughout the main hall of the castle-like mansion flickered as a swirl of energy spun around the room to coalesce into a large stone, protruding from which was part of a blade of a sword with a bejeweled hilt. Beside the stone was a round table with chairs set to seat eight people.

The incantation continued, "From the tears of ten thousand maidens who buried their heroes; fill to overflowing, food sufficient to cover this table. Manifest meat, bread, and wine sufficient for the celebration of the return of King Arthur, his wife Guinevere and selected Knights of the round-table."

Again the energy swirled so forcefully candles flickered. Some were extinguished and reignited on their own as food appeared on the table. The table was laden with succulent venison dripping mead rivulets, roasted pig and fowl on silver platters with wine in silver carafes. The smell of fresh-baked bread permeated the room and in the middle of the table sat a bejeweled golden chalice filled with blood-red wine.

Before he manifested his Arthurian guests, Merlyn inspected the food, wine and stone that he had manifested and became aware of a slight tremor in all the enchanted items. It was but a small vibration yet he became concerned these material things might begin to dissolve. This cannot happen he thought. I will make these creations permanent so they cannot dissolve and disappear.

Oh, Annwn, magical cauldron from the Otherworld bring to me the original items, the stone, the wood for the tables and chairs, the tablecloth, the silver plates and platters the golden chalice and the food. I do not want them to vibrate in and out of existence.

Make them permanent and as well let my Arthurian guests be made permanent as they manifest.

A dark grey hooded face appeared floating above the cauldron, spoke; "I must do as you bid for you are my master but are you aware of the consequence of shifting this much energy from one space-time to another.

Merlyn stood speechless for a minute as his face reddened and he clenched his fists; "STUPID, IMPUDENT, IMBECILE." He screamed, "I did not cast a spell on that poor dumb antique dealer and drag you across an ocean so that you could question what I want. I want these things and the people from Camelot to be permanently in my world. Annwn replied, "Yes, Merlyn as you wish."

One by one the Knights manifested and sat at the table each according to their nameplates. Sir Lancelot, his son Sir Galahad, Sir Gawain, Sir Percival, finally Sir Gareth. All five rose to greet King Arthur who was followed by Lady Guinevere. She bowed slightly to acknowledge the six standing men and was seated.

As the group took their seats the hall was filled with sounds of laughter and chatter and the clinking of glasses as the party got underway. From another part of the castle, a small group of musicians, lyre, flute and drum took up a place in a corner of the hall and began playing.

This surprised Merlyn as did a servant from the kitchen carrying a pitcher of mead and some clay-fired mugs. These additions were appropriate to the scene unfolding before Merlyn; however, he began to feel uneasy, how could these things manifest by themselves? They had not been requested.

Just then the double doors leading to a courtyard sprang open. Two men in fifth-century soldiers' uniforms stepped into the doorway and saluted a short grey-haired man who entered the hall. He was dressed in a long dark monk's robe with a tall cylindrical hat of the same colour and carried a staff.

Merlyn could see something had gone very wrong and started towards the caldron to set things right. King Arthur spoke out; "Merlin, so glad you could join us!" Looking straight at the 21st. century Merlyn, Arthur continued; "You boy! Go and bring Merlin a chair and a plate. Quickly!"

Merlyn looked about, confused. He spoke; "But; but this cannot be! I created all of this. I am not a servant here."

Lancelot stood drawing his sword; "Shall I dispatch this lowly cur, my Lord and find us a proper servant from the kitchen.

Again, a dark hooded face appeared floating above the cauldron. Annwn spoke; "Welcome to Camelot Master. And as you requested; permanently."

Bio: Neall Ryon

Born in 1940 Neall Ryon can truly be considered a Renaissance man. Since he heard Socrates' maxim that an unexamined life is a wasted life, Neall has focused on seeking to understand life.

Apart from being a perennial student of life, his work history includes a variety of careers as a research manager, a business consultant, a business owner, a teacher, a husband, a father, a wanderer, a poet and for a year the co-host of a radio show; World Poetry Café. His poem; *"Easter Parade"* was selected to be included among the 150 poems celebrating Canada's 150th Birthday in the collective book *Multicultural Creative Writing Collection*.

In his travels throughout the world and his wanderings through a life of adventure he sought to answer the question; "What is there in life that is real and meaningful?" He concluded that a meaningful path was not to be found in the experiences of life's external offerings but in seeking out the truth that hides within each of us … our inner spirit, our Soul. The conclusion is it is not what you do in life that gives it meaning, it's the passion with which you live it.

Copyright © 2023 Neall Ryon.

Contact and a few recent examples of his poetry can be found at

www.fromtheotherside.ca